Last

Summer

I Went

Swimming

Last
Summer
I Went
Swimming

a novel by

Craig Joseph Danner

CRISPIN/HAMMER

HOOD RIVER • SEATTLE

LAST SUMMER I WENT SWIMMING.
Copyright © 2013 by Craig Joseph Danner

Publisher's Cataloging-in-Publication Data
Danner, Craig Joseph
  Last Summer I Went Swimming/
  Craig Joseph Danner.—1st ed.
  p. cm.
  ISBN 987-0-9706405-2-9 (pb)
I. Title.
Library of Congress Control Number: 2011900405
813'.54—dc21

CRISPIN/HAMMER PUBLISHING COMPANY
P.O. BOX 1160
HOOD RIVER, OREGON 97031 USA
www.crispinhammer.com

*—to my old friend Andy,
and his wonderful parents,
Thomas and Donna...*

*...and to Stacey Alyson Danner,
newly and forever beloved*

this summer I went swimming
this summer I might have drowned
but I held my breath and I kicked my feet
and I moved my arms around
—*Loudon Wainwright III*
The Swimming Song

Part One

smiling with

a battered grin

of broken wood and stone

of bones of fish bleached

toothy white

with sand and pebbled rocks that laugh

like clapping hands

smothered in the draining strait, the water cold and treacherous. For years I've struggled with this poem, an epic tale of love and death, of blood and sex and wounded hearts, of loneliness and suffering. But I have to get through this part first, the innocence and mother's milk: a girl and boy, an island shore; a verse with hints of saccharine. I am my own protagonist, and Jana is the girl-next-door, lives down a couple summer homes; we'd meet out in the mornings when we're maybe seven-eight years old. We'd walk around the rocky Point, the island's cleft and jutting chin, exploring all her jagged scars, the fissures choked with kelp and logs, the wrinkles that betray her age, the island twice as old as God.

The logs get battered every tide, washed from rafts of clear-cut trees, collected over years and years, the harvested Olympic range. We'd balance on these jumbled logs, riding those that roll and buck, playing this forbidden game my father said was dangerous. Having reached the other side, we'd stand on top of solid rock, safely past these snarling logs with barkless teeth bared snapping just to bite a careless foot or hand, their spit all salty foam and sand.

We'd scamper further down the shore to scout the Doctor's empty beach: a hundred yards of mud and sand all pocked so that the clams can breathe. It's the only beach the island wears, like a bauble round her granite neck: a silty jewel of jetsam, or the slobber of her ocean-child. We'd check then if the coast was clear, to trespass on the Doctor's land; Jana always just ahead, and wishing that I weren't so scared. She'd stop all-of-a-suddenly, scanning for the enemy, the beach was naked to the waist, the tide out playing in the sand.

"Stop!" Jana said, because there's Annie walking on the shore; the beach hers now that she's the Doctor's blind and nasty widow-witch. My father once tried to explain how the Doctor didn't treat the sick; he'd struggled to find easy words describing a pathologist. "He cuts up people when they die, to find out what was wrong with them," and that was all it took to fill the minds of children five years old. We'd see his widow sitting on a log high on the sandy beach; we figured that she'd killed him for a vastly huge inheritance. She was shaped like sand inside her clothes, with whiskers on her chin and nose, and Jana grabbed me by the arm to shield me from potential harm. We watched from fifty yards away as Annie stood up cautiously, her gray hair tangled in the breeze, her ageless dress down past her knees. She walked about ten feet and stooped, then slowly stood upright again; she'd snatched up something from the sand and held it in her wrinkled hands.

"I told you," Jana whispered, "she's just pretending to be blind."

We watched the Doctor's widow walking slowly back up to her house: her cottage anchoring the Point, its windows staring back at us. Every now and then a cat went scampering across her path; she kept a pride of feral beasts, all mangy orange and calico. Annie walked as slow as night, like racing with the moon and stars, but once she finally disappeared, then Jana led the way again. We climbed down to the sandy beach, with Jana unafraid, at least, the witch might plan some sneak attack; might drown us in the pit we'd made, digging treasure from the Doctor's sand.

maybe

she is waiting

for the nails to pierce her feet and hands

a god of stone

with patient arms

of softly wrinkled rock and sand

that cut and cross and sometimes

wrap the ocean as it suckles

cold and fitful

at her salty breast

    I know this island very well, each summer since I was a boy: exploring every nook and cranny back so many years ago. The island's old and gray and she can hold the ocean in her lap: the tide that, like a small child, picks at scraps of ancient wooden floats, the bits of boats and broken toys left lying in her granite folds. The island sits and lets the water rock and nurse against her warmth, and the ocean's sleepy surface mirrors the grayness of her face and hair, the grayness of the early sky so cloudy with its quilt of rain. I remember this one morning, with the stillness like time disappeared: the water sleeping late and deep, all cuddled in the island's lap. We walked along the island's skirt, picked drift-wood from the tidal pools, tucked pieces in a burlap sack that smelled of salty moss and mold.

The smells were always strong back then, sucked deep in through a thumb-small nose, the musty odor of buried treasure, the scent of rotting wood and gold. A mist fell on the burlap bag, beading on its oily fur, drifted down on Jana's hair, a veil like softly polished dust. She bent to pick up something resting quiet in a fold of rock, and the veil spilled down like shattered glass, went scattered over everything. It was all that broke the morning silence: Jana's black and shiny hair, falling down about her face, she flipped it back behind an ear. She stood and held a piece of driftwood cradled in her slender hands; called for me to look and see the image staring back at her.

"Look at this," she said, and held the soggy driftwood out to me; not letting go herself so that together we examined it. There in the tangled branches she was pointing out a face she saw: a wrinkled nose, a withered eye, the roots were like Medusa's hair. The mouth showed a sad broken grin from twisted grain that dripped, she said, like tears across the weathered cheeks: a dying woman, sad and weak. We were probably just nine years old, our hands were still the same small size; I watched hers move across the wood, so lightly brushed against my own. It felt all light and spidery, our hands together tangled up; not sure which ones were mine or hers all flowing through the weathered wood. And suddenly she took the wood and threw it out into the tide; the soft splash sounding muffled by the swirling mist still thick and gray. I looked into her eyes then, and she smiled and gave me back my hands; attaching them to each wrist so that I could now resume command. Perhaps I should have known the deep significance of what she'd done: throwing back what wasn't hers, just borrowed from the ocean-child. Blindly, though, I smiled back, testing fingers left and right, then let her wrap them up in hers, as warm and soft as just-baked bread.

We made this search each morning, a chore to gather wood and bark; we'd lay the pieces out in rows to dry out when the sun was hot. A good big chunk of bark might burn for hours in an evening fire, simmering to bright red coals that tease the other burning logs. We'd empty out our burlap bag, divide things in disordered lines, examine all the treasures found, the fishnet scraps and Styrofoam. That morning brought a wooden float with specks of paint like bright blue sky; that morning, though, the sky was gray: a fog horn intermittently. We left our bag out by the log for years has rested on the Point, its barkless wood as smooth as skin, the color bright as porcelain. I imagine what the storm was like that washed this log up on the rocks: it's solid as the rock itself, the trunk thick as an elephant. The storm must have been wonderful, the breakers big as tidal waves; the sky as dark as diesel smoke, the wind a constant hurricane. I'd always wished to see these storms that only come in winter months, but I'm just here in the summer when my father isn't teaching school. Jana told me stories, though; her family lived here all year round: her mother and her older brother, father dead a couple years. She said the storms were beautiful, but mostly there was steady rain: the cedars and the Douglas fir all wet and dripping constantly.

Jana then walked past me where I leaned against the mist-damp log, went to stand out on the Point, a bone-white patch of barnacles. I watched her dare the sleepy tide to lap against her tennis shoes; the water yawning slowly with a touch of foam against its lips. The water reached for Jana as if hungered by her milky smell, and she teased it with her feet that gripped so tightly to the rocky shore. Then suddenly she ran to me, pulled us both out on the Point, then made us do a little dance to keep our shoes from getting wet. The water breathed asthmatically, coughing foam on sneakered toes, then made a bigger effort so that suddenly we're ankle deep. It was August and quite warm enough, even with the misty gray, and the tide now crashing through our shoes would warm like fresh-cooked porridge and make bubbles with each step we'd take. I was suddenly quite hungry since I hadn't had my breakfast yet; crept crashing past my father sleeping quiet in his too-big bed. He'd turned as I'd gone shoeless past, his bedroom open to the draft; I'd started, jumping back a foot; anxious of his morning smile like strange sounds in the yard at night. I watched his face turn toward me, then rest limply on his pillow case, his mouth still straight with deepest sleep, dwarfed by his pillow's fluffiness. My father was a quiet man, but I'd always been afraid of him: had custody at Christmas break, then three months in the summer time. I finally found the strength to breathe, I watched his eyes move in his sleep; they raced inside his horrid dreams of grading papers late at night. He hugged the

big bed's second pillow snugly up against his chest,
and his body moved against it with the rhythm of his
bedside clock. I moved then quickly past his door, the
stairs moaned underneath my socks, the living room in
dark brown light, like syrup poured on griddle cakes.

I was hungry and was thinking we should fix ourselves some cereal; my father slept till nine or ten so
Jana often ate with me. We were standing far out on
the Point, tennis shoes were soaking wet, wrapped up
in the island's shroud, the light the shade of honeydew.
Both of us stared out to sea, I felt the fog horn stun the
mist, when close in on the gasping water, suddenly
three heads appeared. We watched six giant nostrils
flare, sucking at the glowing air: sea lions with their big
brown eyes, as round and clear as bowls of broth. Their
earless heads, like whiskered apples, bobbed there with
the ocean swells, watching me and Jana standing big-
eyed staring back at them. We listened to the deep low
growl, their nostrils gulping at the air; perhaps to help
the ocean-child to fill its lungs the size of whales. Our
little dancing game had stopped, both of us as still as
space, when suddenly the sun came out and splashed
all over everything. It surfaced from its depth of cloud to
silhouette the lions' heads, drawing lines around the salt
dripped slickly down their whiskered snouts. I turned
my head, the light so bright, shining solid with my eyes

still wide; I saw my father far behind us, standing just below the house. I watched as he brought out a gun, a pistol from his side pocket: we were such an easy target standing close and backlit by the sun. It seemed all too familiar, like some thriller sitting in his lap; he'd sometimes read aloud to me, whatever book was gathered there. His lap was much too small so I'd sit hunched-up close by on the floor; listen as he cracked the spine of paperbacks he'd bought in town. And having seen him draw this gun, I braced myself for searing pain; grabbing tight to Jana's sleeve, I was waiting to see bullet holes. But as he raised the pistol up, it changed into a naked hand: a soft wave from his slender hip, a cursory acknowledgement. I turned back to the sea lions, but they'd sunk back down beneath the waves, and the clouds were parting wider so the water sparkled bright and gay. Jana saw my father then, and waved back to him cautiously; she knew as well as I not to go making any sudden moves. We started off around the Point, still further from the beach and house; could feel my father's quiet stare land wet against my sunburned neck. The image of the lions had been burned into my retinas, and so it danced before my eyes, the flaring nostrils gaping wide, the three heads floating motionless like resting on a pool of oil, more volatile than I could know.

buried in the pitted sand
cookies poisoned on a plate
feeding dogfish
bloody salmon
entrails
from a fisherman
       fighting, thrashing
muddy bottomed
periwinkles underfoot
growing up from small to large, knocking heads against
the sand; we'd eat my father's sandwiches, wade freezing in the tidal pools: the goose-bumps tight against our
chests, the breeze touching the cold, cold water like dia-
monds studded to our skin.

Always, when I arrived each summer, I'd find Jana somewhere on the beach; not waiting but just there so that each summer was connected, time unbroken from the summer past. The first day I'd feel insecure, wonder if she's still around, wonder if she'd still consider playing with a geek my size. We wouldn't say hello when I'd first find her busy on the Point: herding rock crabs with a stick, her back bent to the task so that she'd only glance at me and smile, the connection made from months before. So after just a half an hour I'd feel like I was home again: Jana still the neighbor girl, still my best and only friend. My father might be watching from the ledge below his bungalow: sitting in a lawn chair with one eye above a mystery. We were safe there on the island, nothing more than just a cut or bruise; not because he watched us, but because we knew enough to never eat the cookies Annie baked: offered shaking deadly as a snake coiled in a paper bag, a tremor in her veiny hand, with dark clouds where she should have eyes.

I remember sitting in the field, above my father's dark red house, tired from splitting wood now I was old enough to wield an ax. The wind rushed from my lungs making a whistle from my fleshy nose so that I had to turn to see: there's just an empty field, as still and green as growing moss. A breeze was moving branches and it felt so good to gulp the air, to suck at it so greedily, the tingling rush of blood up to my head like breath on glowing coals. I remember it like yesterday, so proud to have to strip my shirt, to raise the ax above my head, displaying to the empty field the hair beneath my arms at last. And I wasn't really hugely fat; no one would turn around and stare; my mother nagged that I should maybe lose about a dozen pounds. The breeze chilled sweat along my back, like standing far out on the Point, mere inches from the little waves: their dainty little ocean spray. The field was such delicious cool, swollen wet with greenery, speckled thick with shade and sun that dappled through the moving trees. The forest crept in from the left, the right side had a line of trees that hid the road that drifted down to the Doctor's little bungalow; where Annie now lived all alone, afraid of nothing anymore, the radio for company.

I was staring down this narrow field, this massive solid slab of rock, watching as the last night's rain went trickling towards the water tank. The tank was stuccoed cement block, a rotting cedar roof on top, endlessly collecting rain that filtered through the rocky moss. It was full of dark and silent water, perfect deathly hiding place; just the spot, we'd whisper, where the Doctor could hide his mistakes. We'd shiver at the thought of bones all cluttered rotting deep below, beneath the rain as old as hell that went to flush the toilet now. We'd stare down through the unlit water, feet against the ladder rungs, the water just the color of the Doctor's dark and searching eyes.

As I sat out in the field, the ax head resting on my shin, I watched as two deer walked by like they didn't know that I was there. They came in from behind the trees that hid the steeply rutted road; I was thinking of a girl from school who one time kind of smiled at me. Trying once to talk to her, she only made this funny face; who, afterwards, passed in the hall, would never look at me again. I watched the deer walk slow as sap, nibbling at the moss and grass, so close that in my mind I saw I touched them with my hands. Jana was behind me then, quiet so she startled me, a hand placed gently on my back so that I jumped a little bit. We watched together as the deer went walking off into the trees, the forest closing round their tails, the rustling of the gentle breeze.

We both stayed quiet for some time while hoping they might reappear, or just enjoying something shared: a doe and fawn across a field, the smell of fresh-split cedar tree. I realized how strange this was, that I should feel so comfortable; I'm fifteen and my best friend is a

girl so quick and beautiful. She was leaning lightly on
my back, offering forbidden fruit: red and crisp inside a
hand that now was smaller than my own.

"Thanks," I said, and took a bite, wiped my hand
against my shorts, turned around to look at Jana backlit by the dancing sun. Long black wisps of Jana's hair
were blazing all around her head; I had to squint to see
her face, her eyes so dark and mischievous.

"Want to go?" she asked, about a trip planned
to the Doctor's lake; our first trip of the summer to
our private little swimming place. It was up a skinny
trail we'd made, the nettles grab our naked knees; the
shallow water of the lake just deep enough to soothe the
sting. The lake was an experiment, the Doctor damned
a seeping spring, to use it as a reservoir to pipe down to
his bungalow. He'd long ago abandoned it because the
distance was too great, so now it was the secret place
we'd go to for a change of pace. The shallow water killed
three trees that wade about a meter deep, stripped of
bark so that they swam less modest than the two of us.
It was different from the ocean, with the bottom soft and
squishy mud; the waves pushed by the forest breeze
might drown a lazy grasshopper. These ripples skirt the
sterile trees, lap against the grassy shore; we'd stretch
out drying in the sun and count the ants and lady bugs.

"Want to go…?" she asked me, and I looked up at

her once again; she'd walked around so that the sun shone brightly on her chest and face. I was still surprised at how she looked, so changed from just nine months before; and yet that felt like yesterday, the fall and winter disappeared.

"I'll need to get my swimming suit," and I had to look the other way, embarrassed by a blushing thought had never yet occurred to me.

"Me too, I guess. I'll be right back," she said this as she turned to go; we both went off our separate ways: I stumbled towards my father's house, and Jana walked off through the woods, exactly where the deer had gone.

The water was like ice, and we crawled gasping to the grassy shore; it melted from our skin the way that frost might turn to morning dew. Jana sat beside me while she pulled at her bikini top; we were red from cold and rough with bumps, the sun just barely hot enough. I was lying in the grass, I had my head propped sideways on my hand; I saw the light spark off the lake, the surface looked like broken glass. I could almost hear the squeal of brakes, the two cars blocking traffic now, the trees all start to rubberneck this silent lake-side accident. They pushed to get a better view, swaying in the gentle breeze; so quiet that I sometimes heard their creaky

moans of sympathy. The warmth pulled over blanket-
like, smoothed the goose-bumps on my arm, and I lay
there blinking at the sun, feeling like I just woke up.

"I'm glad you're back," she said as she wiped water
gently from my side.

She leaned her back into the grass, her face up to
the bright blue sky; I watched her eyes close to the sun,
her mouth perfect a half-a-smile. We were quiet for
the longest time, and I watched the profile of her face;
beyond her were the tops of trees, swaying like the
flames on top the candles of a birthday cake. It was the
ocean blowing at the candles, pouting little birthday-
child, but the forest filtered out its breath so that we
hardly felt it there. The breeze deep in the grass was
just a kiss wet from the Doctor's lake, though it pulled
the covers from my shoulders, shook me with a sudden
chill. I closed my eyes against this kiss, laid quiet in the
sparkling black; the only thing I felt was Jana's soothing
hand against my side, pulling up the fallen warmth, the
blanket off my grassy bed.

"I miss you when you're gone," she said. "Winters
here are dull as death."

Her hand was on my side again, her fingers brushed
across my trunks; she'd always been a touchy one, but
never touched in such a way to get me thinking certain
thoughts. I had to roll onto my front to hide my unex-

pected shame; I was mortified by my response, my sense this was incestuous. She stroked the backside of my thighs, her fingertips exploring flesh; a sound escaped deep from my throat; no one had ever touched like that. And just like every husky kid, I knew the taste of ridicule; there was not a chance she really wanted what her hand was groping for. I clamped my thighs together tight, flexed the muscles of my butt, didn't dare to move or breathe, my lust hard pressed against the grass. I was waiting for the kind of laugh that let's me know I've been a fool, the signal that this marked the end of summers with the neighbor girl. But she didn't make that snorting sound I'd heard when kids were being cruel; she only took her hand away, then bent to whisper in my ear. Her breath was pleasant sweet-and-sour, the faintest hint of buttermilk.

"Just wanted to find out if you're as glad as I am that you're back."

like a metaphor
it writes itself
poetic loss of innocence
just thinking
  the old woman says
the trees as naked
as the fish
swimming in the tidal pool
it's not an awful sight at all
the water warm as Popsicles
So we'd climb out of the ocean; Jana's skin would
smooth as slow as mine, and we'd lie out in the sun and
watch the tiny waves and hermit crabs. It was sunny

when it didn't rain, when all the clouds would slide away. We'd sun ourselves all afternoon on the beach below my father's house, sitting in a curve of rock as gentle as the sun was hot. We'd take my father's little boat, drifts of light blue two-stroke smoke; we'd putter to the island sitting lonely off our rocky Point. There was just a single tree but lots of rocks for us to lie upon; Jana dares us both to jump, the lee side cliff five meters high. The mornings were much cooler, so we couldn't sit still very long, and we'd walk along the Promenade out past the cliffs of Cable Bay. Sometimes, when the tide was up, we'd get stuck on a jutting rock: climb hands and knees along a bluff to keep our shoes from getting wet.

And I'd always had a thing for food, and Jana loved to exercise; we'd compromise and ride our bikes the four miles to the grocery store. The store was like the island's heart, though nothing ever happens much; I'd sit and eat a maple bar while Jana sipped a diet pop. A cloud of dust would follow Mrs. Leason's car into the lot: a faded gray Mercedes pocked with rusty chips and fender dents. She'd climb from the convertible, dust settling on the leather seats; she was well into her eighties, though she drove it like a maniac. She always liked to tease me about spending so much time with girls; "Such a naughty boy," she'd say, then grab me by a love-handle. Mrs. Leason shuffled in, strained against the storefront door, would chat with Mrs. Bishop as her weekly quart of skim got warm.

The island rested weekdays, every Wednesday when the store was closed, as Mr. Bishop cleaned the windows, Mrs. Bishop mopped the floors. On Wednesdays we might bike right past, a quick wave to the grocery man: his hand already overhead, his squeegee streaking window panes. Our tires on the pavement, we would ride up to the island's bluffs, to stop and say hello to the nice man who shot the puppy dog. It's uphill to the old man's house, a sagging little cedar shack; we lean our bikes against the fence, the loose boards where the dog was shot. It really was an accident, just trying to scare a tourist off; he didn't see the damn thing till the brown grass started turning red. The tourist had been trespassing, the old man owns the road and all, with signs up every twenty yards all threatening the wrath of God. And how was he to know the fool had brought along his poodle dog? Sniffing round the fence while running twenty yards in front of him. Both men had been shaken up, the trespassed and the trespasser; the dog was buried near the fence, the shotgun buried next to it. The tourist made the old man tea, his tremor worse than ever now; the noise and blood enough to knock the stuffing out of anyone. I still can't quite imagine how the two men could have reconciled, but every year the tourist came to visit for an afternoon.

We'd stop and talk and maybe drink a splash of water from his tap, the mountain back behind his house was still a little distance off. His road became a dusty trail all rutted from the logging trucks; years since they had cleared the top of trees a hundred meters up. The island's pate had long been just a crown of old-growth stubble stumps, of manzanita bushes and a view of every compass point. The old man winked at me and said that we'd be all alone on top; just the wind and bushes and the seagulls there to spy on us. We'd lean our bikes against his fence, then walk up the neglected road; the dust beneath our tennis shoes made little clouds to walk upon. The steepest part was at the end, and I'd have to stop to catch my breath; better, though, than when I'd first arrived a couple weeks before. I still can hear the bushes crackle, leaves dry from a rainless month; the sun as warm as tea with milk, the sky without a touch of white. As we'd come out on the top, we'd look out past the sea of stumps, with water all around us and a light smog over Bellingham. There were mountain ranges east and west, snow still on the highest peaks; freighters cruised the dark blue water, the tiny spots of pleasure boats.

We shared a stump, just big enough, my arms

stretched tight around my knees; the breeze still smelled of ocean salt brought filtered through the cedar trees. Jana's hair blew helter-skelter, streamers from a paper kite; I was winded from the last steep pitch, my arms and forehead damp with sweat. Lots of time was spent this way, drying after getting wet: rocks and stumps and grassy slopes, the cool breeze and the solar warmth. Jana's shoulder touching mine, close-up on the giant stump, I felt her scattered dancing hair start tickling against my neck.

"Do you every cry?" she asked. "I don't mean when you hurt yourself. But sometimes in the winter, when it rains and rains for days and days...."

"I haven't cried since I was small," something I learned years before: fat boy tears just make the taunting that much more unbearable. She turned her face to look at me: sun and warmth and ocean breeze, her smile as sweet and sad as water spilling down a mountain stream. Her slender hand against my knee, she pushed until she stood up straight, then pulled me up beside her so we stood together balancing.

"We're the very top," she said, with nothing taller than our heads; she took my right hand in her left and pulled me down the mountain slope. Crashing through the manzanita scratching at my sunburned thighs, she dragged me towards the bluff's edge where we watched the traffic far below. I was wondering about this girl and what she really thought of me; my mother bought me diet pop and pricey acne medicines. Resting on the breezy slope, we planted elbows in the grass, watched the mid-day ferry once more navigate the narrow pass. She was fighting an out-going tide, boiling through the churning foam; coming round a corner she'd sound warnings to the pleasure craft. Three short blasts came from her horn, so sudden that they startled me; deep and loud as thunder claps from lightning half-a-mile away.

"I love it when she does that," she said, "when I feel it deep inside of me. It makes the world seem far more real."

I sat up then and crossed my legs and looked into the paper sack, the lunch her mother made for us, the yoghurt and the carrot sticks. But her mother thought of me as well, and packed a couple extra things: a bag of chips, some cherry pie, two peanut butter sandwiches. Jana rolled onto her side, her head propped on an elbowed hand, looking up the slope at me while I rummaged through the lunch supplies. She reached a hand to straighten out the wide legs of my cotton shorts, laughing when I realized what parts of me were hanging out.

The ferry was an older one, not pretty like she used to be; they'd cut her down the middle to increase her car capacity. The scars were freshly painted, but she now looked rather dachshund-like; she'd churn around the second corner, blast her horn a few more times. I could feel it just as Jana said, my breast-bone nearly rattling; Jana rolled onto her back, now crucified against the grass.

"Have you ever felt all numb inside? Like your body's full of novocaine?" And she didn't give me time to answer, but scooted up the hill to me. "I want to show you something, but you have to promise not to tell."

"Cross my heart and hope to die. Stick a needle in my eye."

She pulled her cotton T-shirt up, showing me a naked breast; just the left one was exposed, the tender nipple stood erect. I'd never seen her breasts before, not since we were eight years old: my father bluntly told us it was time to put our swim suits on. Her breast was just a little thing, a scoop on top an ice-cream cone, the nipple like a maraschino, flesh smooth and symmetrical. The only imperfection was a two-inch bright red jagged scar that tore across the untanned skin like blood-stains on a drift of snow. She watched me as I slowly reached to feel the firm and ropy scar; felt the thick and shiny wound I ran my fingertip along. She pulled her T-shirt down again and tucked it in her canvas shorts, then stared off toward the ferry that was sailing off across the strait.

"I did it with a piece of glass, and I didn't feel a thing," she said, and I tried then to imagine how she'd managed such an accident. She'd kicked her shoes off somewhere, and she combed the dry grass with her toes; suddenly she's laughing like this all has been hysterical. She sat up quick and pushed me over, pinned my shoulders to the ground, swung her head then back and forth, her long hair tickling my nose.

"Let's go back," she whispered, then she crawled away to find her shoes, and as we walked back up the hill I wondered if I knew this girl.

Of course, it was down hill from there, riding off the mountainside; our bikes pulled from the old man's yard, slowing for the graveled curves. It was just a quarter hour till we're gliding past the Bishops' store: windows clean, a cardboard sign, apologizing that they're closed. We crossed the island's highway that's so slow it has no painted line; took the corner at a lean, the road that finally takes us home. It's paved up to the golf course, where we sometimes caught a glimpse of deer, wandering the shabby course, the greens all brown from lack of rain. From that point on the road was gravel, once a year was sprayed with oil; I watched a line of dust form from

the back of Jana's fendered tire. The trees create a canopy,
the sun streaked through the greenery; the dust she made
seemed like a wall that crumbled as she pedaled on. The
gravel snaked around some curves, then down and up
a little hill where I'd get off to push my bike while Jana
bravely pedaled on. The road would finally split in two,
with one fork to my father's house: for months he'd sit
and read while missing grading papers late at night. The
other fork goes to the right down to the Doctor's bungalow: Annie so pathetic with her feral cats and baggy
clothes.

"Let's go let her know," she said, while closing up
the metal box; Jana looked and found that Annie hadn't
gotten any mail. She checked her mailbox everyday,
with Annie now too old and frail; she'd scold her not to
climb the road and risk another tumbling fall. The road
is steep with mud and rocks and rotting leaves from
years before; we'd walk our bikes ourselves or risk a
broken bone or bloody nose. My father's box contained
a letter mother had addressed to me; I stuffed it in a
pocket so my father wouldn't want to see.

"Sure," I said, and pushed my bike off down the
steep mud-brittle road.

She was a witch, we always thought, the mis-
tress of the Doctor's house, who loved a man whose

hands had been where no one's hands should ever go. Every Monday she did laundry, clothes hung even in the rain; she fed her dozen cats the scraps of dead things every afternoon. The cats were orange and hairless beasts, inbred to the nth degree, and all this time the Doctor's sheep kept dying in the summer heat, rank with long neglected wool, forgotten by a doctor who took patients only stiff and cold. Annie's hands would tremble, just enough to give her thoughts away, while offering her treats of death all spread out pretty on a plate. But she melted when the Doctor died, her wicked image sizzling down: now nothing but a broom and dress with which she wiped her opaque eyes. Now Jana fetched her daily mail and drank the woman's milky tea: nibbled biscuits freshly baked that wouldn't cause a tummy ache.

There was music from a radio; I could hear it through the metal screen that kept the cats outside the house; could hear the *ting* of metal mesh pulled stuck off of a sharpened claw. We walked into her yard, all-of-a-sudden all the cats are gone; scattered through the bushes like a crowd of naked poltergeists. Jana knocked against the screen, then opened it familiarly; she pulled me in behind her so the screen slammed bounding back in place. Embarrassed how it startled me, as common as a winter sneeze; I knew her cottage well enough, but never been inside before. And when I turned back from the door, Annie's holding Jana's hand.

"The tea's just made," she said, and led us blindly through the kitchen door, past the Doctor's study, and then down a dark and narrow hall. We sat down in her living room, the sun split by the window panes; we sipped and brushed the crumbs back in the creases of her davenport, thinking she would never know.

rain and water
drowned the fire
the ocean spits out wood and rocks
like broken teeth
a barroom fight
the barmaid calling in the cops
      woke the island in the mornings
waves beat soft against the stone
blackened eyes and dirty elbows
nothing that won't sometime heal
if somehow given time enough
you stop swimming
only when you're tired
very tired. She said,

    "I was just lying there, still in bed. It was kind of
cold in my room, and I liked how warm it was. I didn't

even hear her come in, and she whispered, *Are you awake, Jana?* And I opened up my eyes and my mother sat beside me on my bed, up near my shoulders so that I sank a little toward her knees. It was beautiful, I really love my room when the sun comes in and shines against the wall. Mom put her fingers against my forehead like she was checking me for fever. The sun was shining on the back of her head, and from where I was it looked like a halo, her hair like black cream. She rubbed her eyes with her hand and I could tell she'd been crying. I could feel the tears on her fingers when she touched my face again and ran them down around my cheek. Then she said, *I love you, Jana.* I could hardly hear her when she said it, and she put her hand against the quilt, pressing on my knees. I closed my eyes, and could smell the bacon from the kitchen, and she left to turn the heat down on the stove."

The island's dress is gray and green and bleached and studded thick with trees: tall but not too tall because the soil is thin over the stone, the solid mass of island bone. The gray is rock, quite beautiful, a mirror of the winter clouds: dark and stormy beasts that threaten nothing more than wind and rain. And the green is what comes with the rain, the soft drops trickling down like tears, like sprinkles on an ice cream cone. The storms that come are beautiful, two lovers all entwined in bed: the island and the stormy sky love quietly but passionate.

The shore is sandy stone and rock, blown smooth and yellowed by the sun; washed clean by constant soothing surf, precipitating pitter-pat. The stone is curved with hollowed places shadowed by the angled sun; curves and cracks and shadows in the summer seeming sensuous. To me the rocks seem feminine, no trace of stray testosterone, no bulging biceps boulders flexing proudly in the pounding surf. The rocks are smooth and comfortable, warm nicely in the summer sun; pleasant just to sit and watch the water and the fishing boats. I sat down in my favorite spot, and watched the tepid tide come in.

I had to move my sneakers back, kicked off because my feet were hot; the tiny spray from six-inch waves was trying hard to get them wet. I don't know why I cared but that they'd float away if I forgot; one at a time like little boats, to drift off crew- and captain-less. There was heavy traffic in the strait: fishing boats and pleasure craft, lazy schooners flapping jibs and barges out of Bellingham. To my left I could see Jana walking just below the Ansleys' cliff, navigating through the rocks, she's drifting slow and aimlessly. She was not the one I'd grown up with, the Jana eight-nine-ten years old; she was still a girl at seventeen, though obviously things had changed. I still can see this image of her, jumping careless rock to rock, crossing balanced on a log, her arms held out from either side. She jumped down from the log onto the gravel of the Ansleys' bay, her long black hair and cheek bones hint that she's one-quarter Indian. There was something in the way she walked that makes me still remember this, that even from a distance she was different from the rest of us. Her steps all seemed so careless, though each log could shift, each rock could slip; a misplaced foot was serious. And yet she wasn't looking down, her face turned towards the sky and clouds.

It was sunny, just like all that summer, waves fighting like cats and dogs; the sound of surf so constant that the rare break between curling swells was loudest that warm afternoon. My ears would ring without the sound, the echo of an empty shell; I watched the schooner rolling by, two masts but just a touch of sail. I squint to see who's at the wheel, it looked like it was just a kid, someone with a father standing coiling rope up in the bow. Envy seems so easy, just a glimpse of sailing father/son, a blue sky filled with scudding clouds, an ocean filled with gentle swell. The pang is instantaneous, the sound of waves on wooden hull, they're on a trip, the two of them, to circumnavigate the globe.

"You're lost again. I can tell."

She startled me, crept up behind, her gentle whisper in my ear.

"Life's rough," I said, "wish I were dead."

"Especially when it's sunny. I can't stand it when it doesn't rain."

Jana sat down next to me, the warm smooth curve beside my own; she leaned her head against the rock, her eyes closed to the glare of sun. She laid her arms across her chest, melting in the stone caress, and suddenly I'm half convinced she's been there with me all along. She saw me sitting on the Point, watching wooden sailing boats, as I had seen her cross the log, balanced with her arms spread out. But really she was here with me, sharing all the thoughts I had; we never had to talk too much, she knew what I was thinking of.

"I don't know why it fascinates," the water crashing on the Point: the tide so anxious to come in, the boats out barely cutting wake.

She said it's like an evening fire, "like sitting warm and quietly," and the waves are like the crackling pitch, bursting from the burning logs. "You can think and dream watching a fire," she said the water was the fire, tide rising as you strike the match that snaps and flares the kindling up. "You watch it catch and flare and then the logs begin to burn as well, and your shoes kicked off are getting wet, but who cares with the sun so hot?" It's so warm you can feel it through, heating up your blood and bones, and the fire's roaring bright and hot, move back your chair a foot or two. You get up then to catch your shoe, floating off into the strait, the tide now hiding half the rocks, as high as it was going to get. Both just settle back a while—the fire and the water—just as someone in an easy chair, belly full of stuffing supper. A log rolls over in the coals, and that last big rock is back again: hidden for at least an hour, off running errands, now returned. The evening ferry blasts a note, the sun dips down below the trees, and you throw another piece of bark on just a pile of glowing coals. That's what she said.

Later on one morning, in the summer we were both eighteen, I met her at her mother's house, watched Mrs. Borden ironing. Jana was in the kitchen, maybe, packing up a picnic lunch; I was helping Mrs. Borden fold an acre of white cotton sheet. I love the smell of just washed clothes, all dried out in the ocean breeze, the laundry room was full of these, her mother the domestic type. Her hair was not as black as Jana's, mixed with strands of gray and white; she wore it long and braided tight, hanging halfway down her back. As we fold the sheet in half, we do the old sheet-folding dance: two steps forward, two steps back, fold it once again in half. Our hands met in the middle, I have helped her do this chore before, and Mrs. Borden looked at me, flashing bright a tender smile. She asked me then to fold some clothes, while she starts touching up some shirts; she pointed to a pile of towels, a basket full of socks and things.

"Henry," Jana's mother said, "I'm sure that you already know, last winter Jana wasn't well, she missed more than a month of school." She had another spell, she said, had stayed in bed for days and days, then stared out of the window with a blank expression on her face. I was listening to Mrs. Borden tell me things I didn't know, while folding hand embroidered towels and mounds of cotton underclothes. I fold a yellow camisole, with no idea that's what it's called; imagined Jana wearing this, all shear and ribbed and edged with lace.

"Depression is a family trait. Her dad committed suicide." She worried for her all the time, except, perhaps, when I'm around. "She's so much better since you're back, seems like her normal self again." She's such a pretty girl, she said, but sad when she forgets to laugh. Suddenly I'm mortified, I'm holding Jana's underpants: pink and blue and yellow briefs with flowers printed round the waist. I wasn't sure what I should do with something that's so intimate, while standing with her mother who's explaining certain facts of life. She trusts me like another son, "I know how Jana cares for you." She was ironing her daughter's blouse

while I was fingering her underwear. The panties were
bikini briefs, hardly any cloth at all; I can't resist to
touch the part that slides between her daughter's legs.
I was nearly overwhelmed then with the urge to put
them to my nose; to get to know the private scent of Jana
Borden's pheromones. I struggled then to fold them flat,
was only halfway through the pile; what does it mean
she cares for me, and why should she get so depressed?
Jana had a will of stone, her temper on an even keel; I'd
always heard her father's death was just a fishing accident. But suddenly a button's pushed, my face still in
a vivid blush; her mother put her iron down, her voice
still sounds matter-of-fact.

"I worry less when you're around. I know that you'll
look after her. But you should let me know if you think
Jana might be acting weird."

it smelled of milk
there in a puddle, spilled
before the frigidaire
mopped up ceremoniously
with rag and towel
      cap and gown
so tonight, with supper
drinking water
milk warmed quickly on the floor
canned spaghetti
garlic toast
suffering without dessert
It was wonderfully hot that day—it seldom ever gets
that way—so even in the woods it's warm, the wind a

pleasant wink and smile. Beneath the roof of firs and
cedars, maples thick with bright green leaves, the trail
up to the Doctor's lake was tunnel-like and filled with
shade. It's the main isle of an old cathedral, congrega-
tion ferns and trees; we walked into the silent forest,
humbled by its majesty. Careful to be quiet, since we
were hoping we might find a deer, in single file we
skirt around the nettles reaching for our knees. We
hoped to find one drinking, maybe, nibbling grass
beside the lake; pretending we don't know the deer
are deep in forest, drinking shade. It was something,
though, for us to do on such a gorgeous perfect day,
finished with my daily chores that don't take much
time anymore.

The sun was streaking through the trees, the
branches moving in the breeze, breaking up the
beams of light so that our shadows flickered like a
silent movie run too slow. The forest floor was fresh
from spring, the water sucked up from the soil; fully
green and succulent like spinach in a salad bowl. It
all looked soft and round and padded comfy as a well
stuffed chair; the greenness hiding thorns and stick-
ers hungry for our arms and legs. The first things that
we both saw when we finally reached the Doctor's
lake, were just the three skeletal trees, wading maybe
ankle deep. They were standing sentry over what we'd

quiet crept up here to see, the deer there by the lake-
side, though we needn't have come silently. The young
doe, lying on its side, already with the belly bloat, was
dead perhaps a couple days: lucky that it didn't smell.
Jana, who touched everything, had nudged it with her
tennis shoe.

"I wonder why it died," she said, while balanced on
her other foot.

Its hide was clean, unmarked with blood, its open
eye was feeding flies; a handful of the nasty things were
crawling on its pretty head. Jana kept on nudging it,
hoping that it might wake up; plenty of them on the
island, hunting banned for many years.

"I'll bet somebody shot it. We could turn it if you
want to know."

Jana stopped her nudging then, convinced it won't be
getting up: dead is dead and doesn't change, no matter
how you bother it. The flies buzzed for a moment more,
formed a cloud above the head, then lit back down upon
the deer, exactly where they were before. Jana's hand
grew tight in mine, she nudged the deer just one more
time; the flies then formed a cloud again, then lit back
down upon the head. She grabbed my hand more force-
fully, squeezing metacarpal bones, and as the flies flew
off again, this death-grip started hurting me.

"You're hurting me," I said, and when she turned

around to glance my way, I saw a look of almost wonder flash across her pretty face.

"A year ago I would have cried," she said, thinking someone shot the deer; killed to satisfy some urge, then left to rot into the earth. "I would have thought it was a crime to kill something so beautiful," felt bad for the loss of something walking gently through the woods.

She turned her head so that she caught the breeze that swam across the lake; her profile outlined by the sun that splashed against her other cheek. "I don't think that it's all right to go shooting poor defenseless deer, but if someone hadn't shot it then we wouldn't see it lying there." She walked away a couple steps, closer to the Doctor's lake; I had to walk around the deer to hear what she was saying next.

"I mean, here I am, and it's beautiful today, and there's this deer lying dead by this lake, and I can touch it with my shoe and know it really exists. I can think about what it looked like when it ran through the bush or maybe where it slept last night. If it wasn't there I never would have had these thoughts, and I never would have known that it existed at all...." She paused. "Things die all the time. I think all deaths have meaning. Even senseless ones."

She was quiet for a little while, resting on an alder

tree: thick trunk leaning slightly out across the water of the lake. We watched the warm soft gusts of air that swept across the water's top, causing little ripple-waves to scamper toward the two of us. It was sweetly warm that afternoon, tingling my spinal cord; I remember being tempted by the chilly water of the lake.

"It's nice being alive now," she said, "being aware of a day like today. My body feels so all-alive. It's really kind of nice."

Many years ago the Doctor built a camp beside the lake: a clearing and a log to sit on, ring of fire-blackened rock. The clearing now was overgrown with long grass that had gone to seed; we crawled out of the tingling water, goose-bumps on our arms and legs. We bent the dry grass over as we leaned ourselves against the log, warming quickly in the sun and drying with the wisp of breeze. It was maybe one or two o'clock, the sun just past the zenith spot; I watched as Jana rummaged through the lunch sack that she'd packed for us: plastic baggied sandwiches, the mandatory carrot sticks, some chocolate cake, potato chips, a navel orange she quickly pierced, her thumbnail through the dimpled flesh.

"Here," she said, and gave me half; I peeled a couple sections off, the juice dripped down on to my chest where hair had just begun to sprout. I put both sections in my mouth, as sweet as cloudless summer days; it burned the inside of my lip, a spot where I had bit myself. She gave me half a sandwich.

"Life is...," she paused, holding her breath, "strange. I don't know. Sometimes I feel I'm just a witness to all this—that it doesn't really matter that I'm here at all. And then other times it's the opposite—as if I'm the very center of the universe—as if everything is here only because of me. It's like if I go to sleep the world disappears, and the only things left are just what's in my dreams. When I die, even my dreams will be gone. There'll be absolutely nothing. Not even black."

She took a bite of her sandwich. "Have you ever been depressed?" she asked, still chewing. "I have. It's awful. I felt like a piece of wood. But there's something about summer. I feel really, really good right now."

I was suddenly in agony, my eyes were flooded thick with tears; the sandwich had a spicy mustard, fumes had gone straight up my nose. I was feeling like an idiot, coughing out moist crumbs of bread; Jana pounding on my back, I'm gasping trying to catch my breath. Jana's gasps were just as hard, her laughter mixed with sympathy, asking if I was okay between her fits of giggling.

"I guess I should have warned you," she said, about the mustard she had used; she put a thumb beneath my eye and brushed a salty tear aside. With her hand still on my face, I finally caught up with my breath; she was looking straight into my eyes and suddenly all serious.

"How come you've never kissed me?"

"Because I wasn't sure you'd want me to." My heart had climbed into my throat, so that I barely said the words.

"That's stupid," she said soft and kind, her hand had slid behind my neck; a gentle pressure from behind that let me know that it was time.

Later, after dinner, I was washing up the forks and plates; my father clearing off the table, asking what I did today. He almost never asked me, so I guessed I looked conspicuous; but what was I supposed to say? That Jana let me kiss her once? "We went up to the lake," I said, but didn't tell him what we did; that Jana let me kiss her mouth, with lips and tongue and everything. "I think somebody's poaching deer," and Jana started tickling me; it took a bit of strength to pin her shoulders down against the grass. "The lake looks pretty full," I said, "the well should do okay this year," and as soon as I let Jana go, she twisting pinched me on the rear. Wrestling round she soon found I was throbbing in my swimming trunks; impishly suggested then we go in for a skinny dip. "There's a tree down by the pump house. I could buck it up for firewood," and I had to shyly turn my back while pulling off my swimming suit. Jana walked into the water, crouched down so she's in neck deep; I made her turn around because I'm mortified that I'm erect. "Annie's looking well," I answered, drying off a dinner plate; my father wiped the drips and crumbs off place mats and the counter top. Jana had a good head start, we raced around the three dead trees; I'm out of breath and shriveled up before I can catch up with her. We were treading water face to face, the water maybe three feet deep; Jana floats in close enough to wrap her legs around my waist. This was nearly overwhelming, glad the Doctor's lake was cold; my father asked if maybe I should try to find a summer job. "There's plenty here to do," I said, could scrape and paint the water tank; Jana came in closer then to wrap her arms around my chest. I couldn't keep us both afloat, my knees sank down into the mud, my head was just above the water, level with her dripping chest. "Annie's sure to have some chores. But you shouldn't ask for any pay," and I was looking then at Jana's breasts: much bigger than they used to be. "Perhaps we could go fishing, son. Seems like we haven't been for years," imagined that her nipples taste like bites of cherry Popsicles. I could see the scar she showed me once, much flatter than it was before; but what I still don't understand is why she should have several more. There were two scars underneath the first, the third still looking red and fresh, and Jana stiffened up a bit, she'd noticed that I'd noticed them. "Sure, Dad, that'd be great," I said, "I've heard it's good at Cable Bay," and once again I ran my finger smoothly over Jana's scar. "You promised that you wouldn't tell." "I haven't said a single word." Jana stood up in the mud and slowly led me to the shore. She told me not to worry, that she'd done this once or twice before, a boy she knew her sophomore year, though that was back two years ago. "Let's go out tomorrow, son. Early, if the weather's nice," and Jana laid down in the grass and pulled me quickly down on top. Afraid that I was hurting her, so small beneath my whalelike bulk, yet as I did the buck and snort she hummed a ditty to herself. And after half a dozen times—well, maybe only two or three—she fit her hip against my back and quickly drifted off to sleep. My father talked of fishing bait, wondered what the cod would bite; I wondered where my father was when his virginity was lost. I listened then to Jana breathing, deep and slow against my side; I'm thinking that I don't exist, unless it's me she's dreaming of.

artesian-like
she's pressurized
bubbles uncontrollably
trips me
beats me
to the ground
laughing, anxious, sleepless nights
she's up before the sun can rise
tapping on my window pane
I'm crusty-eyed and stumbling as we walk along the
dark gray rocks, watching as the dawning sky turned
purple into blue and white. It was chilly on these early
mornings, even with the weather nice. Her hand felt nice

all wrapped in mine out walking on the Promenade, a long straight stretch of sloping rock, the ocean cuddled up to it.

The morning tide was sleepy still, was yawning almost constantly, the surface smooth as teenage skin, a scattering of blemishes. The tidal swells don't break in waves, but push themselves against the rock, and I was listening to Jana as she rushing told me all her thoughts, the thoughts that kept her up all night: imagining a bright blue sky, the color of an iris flower; how now and then she felt she had the sure sign of a heart attack, a pounding flutter in her chest, a sense of being short of breath. She'd been thinking of coincidence, the odds of something happening, the likelihood her house might just be crushed flat by a satellite. She told me once how small she felt, compared to all the universe; how sometimes when her eyes were closed she thought she knew what God looked like. The night before she'd barely slept, but when she did she'd had a dream: a bright light shone upon her showing she was now the chosen one. Her trembling woke her from the dream, her sheets damp from a broken sweat, she'd had to pull her night gown off to dry between her sweating breasts. She couldn't get to sleep again, lay restless on her rumpled bed, then wandered through the quiet house and out into the summer night. All she'd felt was loneliness while staring at the speckled sky, listening to tiny crabs go scratching round the tidal pools. She thought then she should wake me so that she could have some company, and she was laughing when she told me how she would have done it earlier: was halfway to my house before she thought to go put on some clothes.

More than just a few times she'd come tapping at my window pane, waking me from stagnant dreams of science test anxiety. I'd pull on clothes found in the dark to join her for a pre-dawn walk; carrying my shoes and socks at sometime around three o'clock. I'd tiptoed past my father's door, listened for his quiet snore, found Jana waiting silent in the shadows of the darkened yard. Stumbling on the rocks and logs, we'd pick our way out to the Point, the ocean like a pot of ink, a black and silken nothingness. While it was dark she'd whisper she was awestruck by the Milky Way; time and time again, she said, it startles her how big it is. She'd name off constellations that nobody's ever seen before; pointing out the shape of trees, the likeness of her grandmother. I was frightened just a little bit, uncertain what to think of this: she's playful but she's serious, and every now and then she'd turn and ask me for another kiss, a hug to chase the chilliness. I'd try to fold her in my arms, certain they're inadequate, fleshy things that lack the strength to bundle up her energy. I'd feel her shake in my embrace, her breath warm on my drafty nape, the thrill of kissing wet and deep, anticipating what comes next.

We were walking on the Promenade, watching stars all disappear; Jana's whisper rising as the color broke across the east, the black and purple start to mix, the birds in the madrona trees begin their nervous twittering. I could better see the shape of rocks all scattered on the Promenade, half the size of little cars parked perched on crumbling cinder blocks. A heron passed us overhead, a shadow of a silhouette; it startled when it saw us so it suddenly swerved off its course, squawked like an asthmatic duck, let a load of bird poop drop that splashed down on the waterfront. Jana was beside herself, doubled in a giggle-fit, laughing so convulsively she had to gasp to catch her breath. Her laughter was infectious, and at first it seemed hilarious: this all-too-early morning walk, this gift laid down in front of us. I was laughing as I watched her crumple helpless to the Promenade, start rolling, laughing, back and forth, her arms wrapped up to hold her sides. I leaned against a good-sized rock, wiped the moisture from my eyes, chuckling between deep breaths while Jana's laughter doesn't die. She went on for another minute, longer than I thought she would, finally stopped her rolling round, rolled over on her hands and knees. She was just about to stand again, when she looked up at me suddenly, then stuck her tongue out like a dog and wagged her tail up in the air. She made a couple yapping barks, then tilted back her head to howl, then rolled again onto her back for one more round of laughing hard.

I couldn't go along this time, was feeling more and more afraid; it wasn't Jana laughing now, but something wrong inside of her. She went on several minutes more, rolled helpless on the Promenade, then finally let her laughing slow, rested quiet on her side. Sitting down beside her, I attempt to fix her tangled hair, listened to her sighing breaths, the last gasps of her giggle-fit. She put her head into my lap, her eyes were wet and rimmed with red, and it was just then that the sun came up and touched its warmth on both of us.

"I'm sorry," she said, whispering, "I'm not sure what is wrong with me."

Her eyes closed and she didn't speak; she suddenly was fast asleep; I ran my fingers through her hair, Medusa-black and beautiful. My finger traced her slender neck, could feel a subtle pulsing beat; I watched her chest rise up and down, her breathing feeling deep and slow. The tension in my shoulders dropped now Jana finally settled down; was not the first she'd scared me with these bouts of laughing lunacy. For days she'd say she doesn't sleep, goes out for walks alone at night; I'd have to talk her out of things, like swimming to Victoria or diving off the island bluffs. I had trouble keeping up with her while bicycling the lonely roads; she'd pedal on as fast she can while keeping up her monologue. She'd tell me all her grand ideas, like how she'll earn three Ph.D.s; she's going to be an astronaut, exploring Mars and Jupiter. And every time we're all alone, she'd ask me to make love again; even then at eighteen I had trouble with the frequency. She'd drag me up the skinny trail, hands exploring in my clothes; we'd lie down by the Doctor's lake, find nettles in my underwear. She'd tell me not to worry, that she knows just when she'll ovulate; that pregnancy's impossible, her period's not due for months. I knew that this was all insane, should buy those little overcoats; but all the condoms sold were up at Mrs. Bishop's grocery store.

Her head still resting in my lap, I squinted at the morning sun; bright light sparkling in my face, the warmth began to penetrate. The water swelled against the rocks, with just a little bit of breeze; could hear the tiny rock crabs scratching, foraging through kelpy weeds. I had to shake my head to try to keep myself from nodding off; Jana'd been this way for weeks, exhausting all my vigilance. Maybe five full minutes passed while Jana napped against my lap; I hadn't moved an inch except to try to shake my grogginess.

Somewhere to the left a ways I heard a sudden scuffling sound, then something splashing in the tide perhaps a dozen yards away. I saw it in the water, just a black mass floating silently; moving like a giant serpent flashing just its dorsal fin. It was moving right along the shore, ten feet from the Promenade, rising with each passing swell, I'd guessed it was a harbor seal. It swam right up in front of us, finally close enough to see: an otter with her head afloat, her thrusting mate clung to her back. She was making little bleating noises, swimming round in circles now, and I watched this floating mounted pair, her mate had got her by the ear. They circled right in front of us, he struggled some to stay on top; she didn't seem too happy but she didn't try to shake him off. This went on for the longest time, was fascinated by it all, the fact it was okay to stare, the lack of any guilt or shame. Maybe five more minutes passed, the otters slowly float away, when Jana opened up her eyes, as if she'd slept for several days. She scrambled up out of my lap, shaking out her tangled hair; she glanced then up and down the beach to see if anyone was there. She helped me to my feet and then she wrapped her arms around my neck; she bit me on the earlobe, then she whispered through her still clenched teeth: "I think we should have sex again."

laughing lapping quietly
this liquid tickle cuddling
these insects stuck in amber jewels
everything so quiet now
we've finally got the water down
       glancing down admiringly
suspended heads above the crib
stimulating mobile toys
the ocean naps all afternoon
The first week in September and the Ansleys were already gone; the power and the phone turned off, the plumbing drained and curtains drawn. We were sitting outside on their cliff, twenty feet above the beach;

already watched the ocean rise to freshen up the tidal pools. The rocks were almost covered, and the water lapped against the logs all piled high against the bank below my father's bungalow. There was just one boat out on the strait, a cargo ferry headed north; the captain's got a lonely voyage: drafty bridge and coffee cup. There was not a drop of wind out there, the ocean just a sleeping child, so even with the rising tide there wasn't any wave at all. We watched it swell against the rock, just nuzzling the jutting Point; smooth as cotton bunting one would make an infant's blanket with.

Jana's gotten quiet now, compared to just the week before; I'd stayed up with her twice all night while she went talking on and on. One night in particular, I couldn't follow half she said; I sat out on the Promenade while she kept pacing back and forth. I must have nodded off a while, remember how she woke me up: unbuttoning my canvas shorts while kneeling naked in the dark. It was maybe two or three a.m., my father thought I was in bed: totally exhausted and she's wanting to make love again. She reached in with a stroking hand, barely waits for my response; moonlight shining on her skin, I'm straddled like a bucking bronc. Her knees must have been battered raw, she just kept galloping along; all the while she cantered she was keeping up a monologue. She'd started on a subject that she'd never touched upon before: the way

her father killed himself, when she was just a little girl.
Her memory of him was vague, a figure maybe dark and
tall; her mother never told her how or why he'd want to
end it all. It wasn't till the year before that Jana's brother
let her know: their father in his fishing boat, not a trace
was ever found. And though the weather wasn't bad,
they thought it was an accident; her mother didn't find
the note until a couple years had passed. She'd found
it in his favorite book, a simple scrap to mark the page;
for years her mother couldn't tell, or risk the life insurance paid. Whenever Jana asked, her mother said her
father was a saint; her brother, ten years older, said he'd
been the strong and silent type. She wondered was he
really dead, or could it all have been a ruse; he'd faked
the sinking of his boat, was hiding on the island still.
He's living off of roots and deer, a rustic cabin that he'd
made; he's hiding somewhere in the woods, he sneaks
to look in after her. Maybe when she's off at school, her
father visits her mom, remaining lovers all along: elabo-
rate insurance scam.

"For God's sake, would you just shut up?!"

It was too late, I was stricken with a vision of her
father's hair: his long and filthy dreadlocks, his emaci-
ated face and hands. His ragged clothes are stitched from
skins of animals he'd trapped and tanned; a foot long
knife hangs from his belt, he hasn't bathed in several

years. Suddenly I had the feeling Jana's father's watching us: hiding in the bushes near, watched his daughter climb on top. His bulging eyes are red and wild, he's strangling his grizzled beard; then Jana said I shouldn't worry, happens to the best sometimes.

"Besides, my knees are getting sore," she said this to console me some, climbing off unsatisfied, a gelding she'd been riding on. I'd barely got my shorts pulled up, to hide my privates' new disgrace, when Jana'd fallen fast asleep, still naked as the moon and stars. I figured she was freezing with the rocks no longer giving heat; she snuggled tight against my side, breathing lightly in my ear. She had one knee across my waist, an arm held heavy to my chest; I couldn't shake the feeling someone's staring at the two of us. I let her sleep for seemed like days, senses all on red alert; wishing she at least was dressed so this could seem more innocent. I finally can't wait anymore, she'd never slept this long before; a couple minutes max and then she's wound up for another day. Gently trying to wake her up, I shook her lightly by the arm; there's no response and suddenly I'm worried that she might have died. Her arm and leg both draped across me felt like they were made of lead; I tried to move the arm away, with rigor mortis setting in. No longer feeling her warm breath, I was trapped inside her death embrace; pushing on her arm again, she only grabbed me tighter yet.

"I'm cold," she mumbled in her sleep: the least she'd said in several weeks.

I forced her arm off roughly then, not sure what had come over me; she'd kept me up for days and nights for fucking warmth and company. I tried to find her underwear, tossed out somewhere in the dark; groping round the logs and rocks, I found a shirt and tennis shoe. Her briefs were waded in a ball, not far from her denim shorts; I had to try to roll them flat to figure out the front and back. I dragged them up around her thighs, she didn't help to lift her butt; her arms were wrapped around herself, slept soundly as a snockered drunk. Inside I'm deeply smoldering, like nothing I'd allowed before; I'd always been the even-tempered-nicest-boy-you've-ever-known. But why'd she have to talk so much? Running on and on and on? Why'd she never ask me if I thought this was a good idea? For weeks now she'd been rattling, never let me answer her; knowing that I'd follow since she had me by the testicles. And what was I supposed to do? Tell her I'm not in the mood? Lock the bathroom door again and watch the hair grow on my palms? All these weeks we're having sex, seems like every chance she gets, never does she

mention that I'm maybe more than just a friend. And
every couple days I'd been receiving letters from my
mom, picking out my courses from the fucking college
catalog. She tells me if she's going to pay, she wants
to get her money's worth; my father barely asked me
where I'd sent my applications in. They act still like they
hate each other, drove me totally insane; Mom's voice
wore an ugly sneer each time she said my father's name.
And all he did was sit and read his stupid pulpy myster-
ies; maybe he might look up if I cut a major artery. Jana's
still completely zonked, finally got her mostly dressed;
brushed the sand from off her knees, tempted just to
leave her there. But Jana was my only friend, even if
she's not in love, using me because there's no one else
around for her to fuck. Deep inside I'd started seething,
must have been adrenaline; I picked her up in both my
arms and took her to her mother's house. Half a mile of
rocky coast, stumbling through the starry dark, I'm dead
before I get her home at sometime around four o'clock.
There was not a dead bolt on the island, no one locked
their doors at night; arms about to fall off I tried slipping
through the door in back. I was careful not to slam the
screen, through the mud room off the hall, wincing at
the floorboard squeaks I was certain Jana's mom would
hear. I placed her gently on her bed, could feel my vertebrae collapse; I hadn't found her other shoe, so didn't

have to take them off. I struggled then to pull the sheets and blankets out from under her; tuck her underneath the quilt made by her mother's grandmother. I turned around to sneak away, made it three steps down the hall; Jana's mom was standing silhouetted by the bathroom door.

"There's nothing wrong," I whispered, "I just think she's finally tuckered out." I was standing close enough to think she'd slap me hard across the mouth. I took another forward step, hoping she would let me pass; all she did was touch my arm, sliding down to squeeze my hand.

"Thanks for taking care of her," and I'm not sure if she's serious. "She's been this way one time before. She'll sleep now for a couple days."

We were resting on the Ansleys' cliff, we'd watched the quiet tide come in; Jana more her normal self, all quiet and contemplative. She was lying flat out on the grass, no part of her was touching me; she'd slept for days and days and I was lonely long before she woke. I was looking the water, as the cargo ferry disappeared; so far away its monster wake would never break against the shore. I was holding in my hand a rock I'd picked up off the Promenade: smooth and shaped just like an egg, as heavy as a paper weight. I wondered

what might hatch from this, might crawl out unexpect-
edly, might look to me for what it needs: a feathered
nest and nourishment. My fingers wrapped around it
like God made it to fit in my hand, and I rolled it off the
Ansleys' cliff, listened to its landing splash. I couldn't
quite imagine what I'd feed a hatchling from a rock,
and watching off across the Point, an eagle landed near
its nest. I watched it thrust its talons forward, grasp
the unsuspecting branch, tuck its feathers neatly in and
settle down to look for lunch. Underneath the eagle's
nest, Annie walked along the path; every now and then
I saw a cat dart out onto the rocks. Her cats don't like
the tide at all, frightened by the tiny waves that strike at
them like baby snakes, their fangs break on the island's
skin. I watched as Annie disappeared, just behind
the eagle's tree, coming out the other side, slowly as
she drinks her tea. We'd sit now with her sometimes,
serving scones fresh on a china plate; I looked then
down at Jana, who was staring up at outer space.

The eagle stretched its wings at last and pounded
off its barkless branch; we both sat up to watch it feeling
something's going to happen now. I could almost hear
the windy noise its wings made while it lifted off, felt
the beating rush of wind that kept the giant bird aloft.
It flew above the water, Jana smiled and rubbed her

tired eyes; the eagle started turning circles round and round a single spot. Then suddenly its wings retract, it rock-like falls out of the sky; just before it hit the water, spread its wings back out again. With talons wide it pulled a salmon startled from the ocean's grasp; wings now flapping madly just to gain some elevation back. The salmon's much too big a fish, bigger than I'd ever caught; flashing as it nips and tucks, the eagle barely holding on. It was like the bird had caught the spot of sun that dances on the waves, flashing now so brilliantly, the talons deep in silvered flesh. Finally the bird let go, barely gained a foot or more; salmon falls back to the ocean, instantly it disappeared. The eagle darted upwards then, weightless with the salmon gone; flew back to its barkless branch, its talons long preceding it. Jana reached and touched my knee, the eagle folding back its wings, staring out across the water, watching for another chance.

"That was quite a fish," she said, then gently pulled her hand away.

"When are you going back?" she asked.

"I've got another couple days." Jana's boat left in the morning, college clear across the state. She had her things already packed, her cases lined up on her bed, lids cracked like a row of clams all ready for Tabasco sauce. I still could see the eagle sitting staring from its branchy perch; Annie far out on the Point, surrounded by her feral cats. I hadn't seen too much of Jana since the night she'd tuckered out; her mother said she'd slept so hard she'd had to change her bedding twice. She must have slept for four days straight, I'd idled round the beach and house, sat and watched my father read, checked the empty mail box.

"Will you come and say good-bye tomorrow?"

"Sure," I said. "When do you leave?"

"The early ferry. Six fifteen."

"I'll come and help you load your bags."

She'd inherited her brother's car, rusty old jalopy thing; he told her she should watch the oil, could maybe use a set of rings. It didn't have to take her far, Pullman's just three hundred miles: across the water, through the pass, great expanse of wheat and grass.

One more time she touched my knee, brushing off some dirt and sand.

"I'm sorry if I acted strange. I'm not sure what comes over me." I told her that I didn't mind, that it kept the summer interesting.

"I'd like it if you'd write sometime."

"I'd like to," was her brief reply.

My mother wrote to me at school, like something

sent in sympathy: study like you promised, dear, in neatly cursive handwriting. When Jana's letter finally came, it was postmarked from the Bishops' store; I was standing in the student hall, reading how she'd bolted home. She wrote how things had not worked out, how nice the island was in fall: the waves were picking up and slamming hard against the rocks and logs. She wondered at how strong it is, the island with its arms of stone, cradling the stricken child, the ocean with its nasty moods. She told me not to worry and that everything would turn out fine; then asked me, if I wouldn't mind, to think of her from time to time.

more than just a tantrum tide
or someone's shaken soda pop
angry fists and trembling rage
from passing caustic rude remarks
      at times she's an unpleasant child
plays with guns and switch-blade knives
painted clouds and crimson mouthed she
whore-like spreads her legs apart
I was watching from the living room, my nose just
inches from the glass; there were howling blasts of wind
outside, the window rattled in the sash. The clouds and
tide were dark as someone's angry hateful glaring look
and I held my breath, so not to steam the glass, afraid

the added pressure might just shatter-crack the window pane, fractionate my vision of the waves pounding across the Point like the histrionic flailing of a raving little six-year-old.

I was not supposed to be here. I should have still been back at school, with my classmates in Geology, the precious geeks in English Lit. But I was here because I had to be, maybe just to see this storm: standing in my father's house with the power and the phone turned off and no one there since months before. I can still recall the musty smell, the dust mites running rampant through the dampness of the carpet threads. The fire in the fireplace just barely touched the winter cold, mostly only sucked out all the warmth straight up the chimney. Wrapped up in a comforter pulled limply from my father's bed, I struggled to stay warm all night against the raging wind and rain. I was there because of Jana's mom, who'd called to say her daughter's gone: clueless for two days, and she was asking can I tell her of some secret place we used to hide, anything she might have said, some letter weighted heavy as the news of an untimely death.

I'd never seen these winter storms that Jana used to talk about, with waves like greedy snatching hands that grab the last sweet on a plate. To me they seemed like angry fists, all bludgeoning and horrible: they strike the island's martyred face, and knock about the logs and sand. The wind had all the trees bent sideways, swaying like they're in a trance, drawn lonely to some voodoo cult of drugged Satanic worshipers. I'd been out in the rain for days, searching through the cuts and scrapes, cautious of the sea moss growing slippery on the winter rocks. The tall trees in the Doctor's woods all dripped till I was soaking wet; chased back to my father's house by darkness in the afternoon. There was no place that I hadn't looked, now days since Jana disappeared; I'd huddled near this smoky fire thinking she might find me here. Jana's mother told me it was stupid not to stay with them: a temporary empty bed, the thought was so disturbing that I had to turn away from her; instantly imagining the smell of Jana's pillowcase, my hip inside her mattress dent, her granny's quilt beneath my chin, as intimate as kissing deep, as love made by the Doctor's lake.

I am staring out the window, nose just inches from the rattled glass, and the wind has made the waves immense, thrusting swollen on the Point, through all the cracks and crevices. The gray rocks are all streaked with green, the sea moss mixed with barnacles, the tender island's warm embrace does nothing now to calm the child. It's barely dawn enough to see, I'd hardly slept at all that night, the early morning grayness is just mirroring the day before, this storm now working overtime. I saw a ghost in front of me, my dim reflection in the glass, the scattered stubble on my chin, a painful pimple on my cheek. It was then I saw her on the Point, standing up to wind and waves, Jana in a long white dress that's soaking wet against her skin. The window glass was stained with rain, the image wasn't very clear, but I know it's her, though stooped and cold; looks like she's aged a hundred years.

I am outside almost instantly, pulling on my tennis shoes, racing through the soggy yard, the matted grass all slippery. I work my way along the ledge, shouting every step or two; she's standing far out on the Point just back from frantic breaking waves. I am not sure if she's seen me yet, though I stop to wave my arms around, and I'm gripped with fear the next wave might just snatch her from the point of land, drag her through the slippery seaweed underneath the turbulence. The rain is beating on my face, and my throat is raw from shouting loud, and I'm scrambling through the slippery logs a hundred yards still left to go. The wind is swallowing my cries, and her face is turned away; I realize my fear is not that she'll be swept into the sea, but that she's not forgiven me. I should have stayed here with her, and I shouldn't have gone off to school; it's all my fault she's so depressed, that I hadn't taken care of her.

Already I am praying that she'll let me have another chance: forgive me for my selfishness, for never giving back to her. I am thirty yards away but still she hasn't turned to face me yet, and she's stooped and bent there in her dress that's soaked and clinging to her skin like arms from some big octopus. Just before I reach her I already know that something's wrong: her hair has lost its shining black, she's short by half a foot or so. She is standing on a patch of rock that's covered thick with barnacles, the sea moss all around her so there's no place she can safely go. She hasn't heard me calling her, the wind out here is twice as loud, and I'm practically right next to her before she knows that I am there. I can't step on the sea moss or I'll slip into the crashing waves, and I reach across to grab her but she's just a bit too far away. Later Annie tells me that she'd heard a voice out in her yard: the sound of someone calling just above this pounding hurricane. She had gone out to investigate, she'd known about the missing girl, had missed her now for days and days, since Jana always brings her mail. She tells me how depressed she'd seemed since coming home from quitting school; she'd serve the girl a cup of tea, then sit in silent misery. She'd heard the voice and gone outside to see if maybe it was her, worried now for days that she has done some stupid foolish thing. Annie's eyes aren't any good, but

her hearing still is sharp and clear, and even with the
wind so loud she knows it's Jana's voice she heard.
She hadn't put her slicker on before she stepped out in
her yard, while Jana's voice had led her on until she
reached the rocky Point. The wind had been so loud
that she had suddenly become confused; unsure which
way to turn so she could get back safely to her yard.
I'd had to reach to grab her hand to pull her past the
slippery moss, just inches from the hands of death, the
greedy grasp of swelling tide.

Part Two

buried in a wooden box
back behind the winter clothes
she stored her glasses, out of date
forgot the dents across her nose
      the closet smells of camphor balls
      like samples in formaldehyde
I climb the steep mud-rutted road
hand inside the yawning box
examining the canceled stamps
checking dates of postal marks
wonder if she's missed me yet
I'm just a little late that day, too long sitting on the
rocks; I'm fetching Annie's mail for her, a chore I'm

not quite used to yet. We might sit near the piano in her sunny cottage living room, outside on bent metal chairs if Annie's feeling up to it. Today we're on the davenport, Annie rocking back and forth; she's like a little kid who's just been scolded to quit fidgeting. I really don't mind doing this, it helps to fill the afternoons; found work at the marina, but it's just a summer morning job. I fold the letter carefully, the paper thin and crinkly; finished reading it aloud, waiting now for her to move. I wonder how it sounds to Annie, must be ringing in her ears: the news read in a young man's voice, from some old-lady friend of hers. The first page went without a hitch, just general news and gossiping: someone fell and broke a hip, another's in a nursing home. The postmark was from Edinburgh, boring stamp of England's queen; the second page was more the same, until the final paragraph. My voice broke as I realized, and Annie stopped her fidgeting; she asked to hear that part again, the news of someone's timely death.

The letter's on the coffee table, and she reaches out a fragile hand; she knows just where to reach because that's where I put them all the time. Her hand is such a claw-like thing, bruised and marked with liver spots, purple veins through thinning skin, every nail is thick and ridged. Her hand has got a funny tremor, some days makes her spill her tea; she picks the letter off the table, carefully unfolding it.

"You'd think that after all these years, I'd forget the way that Maggy smelled." She holds the letter to her nose, I hear her gently sniff the note. Maggy is a friend from home, she's known her sixty years or more; Annie hasn't seen her since she moved here fifty years ago. But every now and then she writes, keeps Annie up on all the news; the letter's closing paragraph says Francie Setter finally died. She lays the letter on her lap, turns her face away from it; smooths it with a trembling hand as if it were a favorite cat.

"Francie taught me Highland Dance," her tone of voice matter-of-fact; the letter said she'd passed away just this side of a century. All that I can do now is just sit and watch as Annie stares; her face is toward the window where the sun shines in the afternoons. If I knew her better I could maybe tender touch her knee; could offer her a little more than feeble moans of sympathy. But even that's impossible, can't bring myself to make a sound, knowing that it must be pounding viciously inside her head. It's a wonder she can stand it now, any second breaking down; hands up to her ears, she'll want to bang her head against the wall. All she does is stare outside through eyes that haven't seen for years, sensing just the ghost of light that tells her if it's night or day.

"Henry, could you make some tea? There are biscuits in the silver tin."

I hear the kettle's whispered whistle, coming down the kitchen hall; Annie put it on to boil when I'd come knocking with her mail. Her hearing's just as good as mine, the kettle's started rumbling: the whistle like a whining jet just moments before taking off. I'm not yet halfway down the hall, the whistle starts crescendoing, its screech is bouncing off the walls so loud the plaster cracks and falls. I'm standing in the kitchen door; the room filled with a scalding fog, my feet still barely under me, tsunami of linoleum. Everything is shaking, I can hear the clanging pots and pans; whistle just keeps building like an onward rushing subway train. Blindly stumbling through the steam, I make it to the kitchen stove, pull the kettle off the burner, roaring whistle disappears.

Like rinsing dust out of an eye, a swollen eardrum rupturing: suddenly the pain is gone, my vision and my hearing clear. I warm the pot with boiling water, measure out the Earl Grey; Annie says there's nothing else worth being so particular.

"Have you ever seen a Highland Dance?" She still sits on the davenport; I've placed the biscuits on a plate, tea poured into china cups. Her tremor seems a bit subdued, she wipes a damp spot on her face; arranged her teacup in a place she won't have trouble finding it.

"It's all so full of energy, and every move is done just so. I loved it as a little girl. Francie danced us all to shame." She slowly starts to get up, though she'd barely had a sip of tea; she reaches blindly for my hand, requesting that I follow her.

"I want to show you something," and she's leading me back down the hall, surprising that her hand's so smooth, skin so soft and dry and warm. She stops before a door I've never seen her open up before, drops my hand and turns the knob, has to push it rather hard. It's dark as night inside the room, curtains hide the window frames; I'm looking over Annie's head, I'm taller by a foot or so. She takes a few steps forward while I stand inside the open door; she's got one hand above her head, she's got it waving back and forth. I'm not sure what she's doing till she finds what she is searching for; gives the cord a tender tug and lights the light bulb overhead.

"Is that enough for you to see?" The bulb is maybe forty watts. "If not I'll pull the curtains back."

The room's full of detritus, like the beach after a winter storm: shelves and tables cluttered deep with driftwood bleached and washed ashore. The light is dim but adequate, casting shadows everywhere; the single bulb swings back and forth so that the tangled shadows swirl. I'm startled by this storage space, it's such a snarling ugly mess; nauseated by the motion, shadows dancing round the room. But slowly then the swinging stops, it's better when my eyes adjust; I'm staring at a cluttered room of things she's picked up off the beach. It's like some kind of studio, a workbench up against a wall, the driftwood scattered everywhere is actually quite orderly. Annie steps up to a table, knows exactly where it's at; she runs her hands along the driftwood, searching for a single piece. I watch her hands explore the wood, it's obvious she knows them all; fingers run through tangled roots all stone-ground by the swelling tide. I'm not sure what to make of this collection of the island's junk; been stepping round it all my life, not even decent firewood. Then Annie makes that sighing sound of someone finally satisfied, her hands around a piece of driftwood stands a half a meter high. She asks me to come look at something no one's ever seen before: she found this lying in the sand a year after her husband died. To her it was a shadow she might just as well have tripped upon, out walking slowly on the beach, her morning constitutional. Dropping slowly to her knees, she dug the sand from all its sides, fought the childish ocean's grasp to hold it solid in her hands. Exploring with her fingertips, she found its varied curves and crooks, she'd cleaned and trimmed and sanded smooth, then cut one end off nice and flat. She's never seen it with her eyes, it's always sat here in the dark; she thought she'd show it to me now because it looks like Highland Dance. I'm not sure what I'm supposed to say, it looks just like a piece of wood; like something floating round for years then washed up on the Doctor's beach. Annie's maybe got a screw loose rattling around inside: put her in Seattle and she'd wander with a shopping cart. But she's just heard that a friend has died, so I try to think of something nice; I tell her that I like the way the grain plays with the subtle light.

"I've wondered what the grain looks like," and she puts the piece of driftwood down, slides it on the table back exactly where she'd got it from. "Let's go finish up our tea, before it gets completely cold." I take a few steps toward the door, and Annie searches for the cord; hand above her head again, she waves to a departing friend.

morning
like most mornings
waking up before the sun can rise
sleep again
wake to find
it's swept across the bedroom floor
warmed the socks behind the door
dirty, but I pull them on
hair shirt for despondent toes
Stumbling to the bathroom I place stockinged feet on
unwashed mat, stand before the toilet tank, watch the
flushing water swirling blue from Mr. Tidybowl. The
bathroom window faces north, a place the sun will

never shine; I run the faucet just enough to splash some water on my face, dig the sand out of my eyes. It must be ten o'clock already, Tuesday mornings off from work: boring stuff like pumping gas for tourists at the public dock. Looking in the bathroom mirror, I'm bleary eyed with cowlicked hair, fingering a tender spot I've found back by my shoulder blade. I'm wondering if Jana cared how fleshy were my upper arms; wonder would she choose me if there'd been some other guys around. There's twice the hair now on my chest, at least a dozen curly sprouts; belly wouldn't be so bad but for the flabby love handles. I can't quite comb my cowlick flat, finally give up in disgust; suddenly can't stand the fact I'm wearing third-day-dirty socks. I pull them off and throw them in the hamper back behind the door, landing on my father's shorts, his limp and faded underwear.

With every step across the grass I'm slaughtering the unaware: yellow heads of dandelions caught between my spreading claws. Like spiders catching butterflies, my toe-webs snag their tender stems; each forward step I strangle them, yanking off their pretty heads.

"Have you had your breakfast yet?" I'm outside by the rocky ledge, walking toward my father oh-so busy with his reading list. I'm in a mood, I'm not sure why; completely unamusable: as if my heart weren't pumping blood, but turpentine and vinegar. It's hard to crack the faintest smile, to greet him with my normal cheer; I'm wishing he were somewhere else so I could have the better chair. The sun is sparkling on the water, fresh breeze coming from the south; the strait is quite a busy place with half a dozen fishing boats. I'm standing right behind him, he is looking through binoculars: sipping tea with honey, on his lap another mystery. I'm not sure what he's looking at, and not sure that I really care; distracted by his bald spot like a spreading plague on top his head. The sun glints off the shiny skin, the freckles scattered here and there; wonder just how many years before I also lose my hair.

"I thought you'd gone to work today, or I'd have left some Cheerios."

I'd rummaged through the kitchen, couldn't find a speck of cereal: just a half an inch of milk, the dry end of a loaf of bread.

"I'm always off on Tuesdays," and I'm not in a forgiving mood, thinking maybe he could think of someone else a time or two.

"I'll cook you up some scrambled eggs."

"There isn't any bread for toast."

"How about some pancakes, then?"

"There isn't any syrup left."

He's still got the binoculars propped up against his spectacles; hasn't stopped his spying on whatever's so damn interesting. He doesn't have the faintest clue when he asks me if I'll scratch his back: a spot he can't quite reach right smack between his narrow shoulder blades. The binoculars drop in his lap, he's leaning forward just a bit, wearing an old T-shirt that was printed for a teachers' strike. I can't see how I can refuse this relatively simple task; half-hearted run my fingers up and down the muscles of his back. He sends me chasing round the itch, *go further right, now lower yet;* then asks me if I'll rub his neck, his shoulders feeling sore and stiff. I can't recall him ever having asked me to do this before; our last show of affection was perhaps when I was six years old. I remember it quite clearly still, this universal ritual: dressed in my pajamas I taste perfume from my mother's lips. They're sitting in the living room, weeks before they finally split; I'm leaning toward my father to impart another good-night kiss. The moment that our lips connect, it's almost like a gun went off: I know without a doubt that I've done something that I shouldn't have. Boys don't kiss their fathers' lips, I know that's what his thinking was; he didn't wince or grimace but I felt an icy awful dread. He didn't offer me a hug, didn't rumple up my hair, didn't bother telling me the rules change every now and then. *Don't forget to brush your teeth,* his smile seemed plenty broad enough; but somehow it was false or dead, I never once kissed him again. And now my hands are on his shoulders, inches from around his neck; muscles feel so stiff and tight I squeeze and still can't make a dent. Expecting him to moan or groan to let me know he's had enough; I wonder if he's human or a robot that's not programmed right. I finally take my hands away, he shrugs his shoulders up and down, turns his head from side to side, says *thanks, I really needed that.*

"There must be something you can eat."

"I'll ride up to the Bishops' store."

"I really thought you'd gone to work."

"Forget it, Dad. It's no big deal."

There's a button on the handlebar, turns the putting engine off, and I push it while I glide along into the gravel parking lot. I'm hoping nothing's wrong with it, my rusty little scooter bike; bought it from a college friend so I could look for summer work. It makes a funny clunking sound while shifting into second gear, wonder if I really got the clutch adjusted properly. I should have bought one from Japan, instead of this Italian thing, but saw one in a foreign flick: exotic and bohemian. And if there weren't a helmet law, I'd wear a little French beret;

I tried to sprout a goatee but I didn't have the facial hair. It was after a semester course on reading beatnik poetry; it wasn't till I bought the bike I found it really wasn't me. The helmet gets tied to the rack, I comb my fingers through my hair; Mrs. Leason's on the porch, grabs quickly for a love-handle.

"Used to ride one just like that," then gives her pinch a little twist. "I used to be an army nurse. Spent three years off in Germany."

She let go of my bruising flesh, careful stepping off the porch, climbs in her Mercedes just as slow as an old lady should. Then she almost hit my scooter as she backs out of the parking lot, spitting dust and gravel as her foot stomps hard against the gas. I go into the little store, Mrs. Bishop says hello: the only one who still thinks Jana's drowning was an accident. She asks me how I'm doing, how I like my new marina job; I tell her that I'm doing fine, the job keeps me from getting bored.

"Jeff is home on leave next week. You two should go out fishing some." I tell her that I'd like that, though I've never really liked her son.

"Tell him to drop by some time," and she rings up my two purchases: a quart of low-fat chocolate milk, a box of stale doughnut gems. I sit out on the wooden bench, shaded by the overhang, waiting for the sugar to correct this awful mood I'm in. I swallow bites of fat and flour, washed down with the chocolate milk: I sit and watch a half an hour, but not a single car goes by.

within her voice
a mountain speaks
threatens daily to erupt
the sound of frightened running feet
      I faintly hear the rumbling sound
      of otters on the Promenade
running from the breaking surf
inches deep and dangerous
it breaks before it hits the rocks
this one wave just like all the rest
It breaks and slaps against the rock that slopes down to
the water's edge, amazed the island puts up with such
constant caustic insolence. The power's on the island's

side, deep within the silent rock; she never lets a sound escape, as patient as a martyred saint. The ocean lets its temper loose against the island's face and breast, beating on it ceaselessly for geologic centuries. And still she's hardly worn more than a healthy looking grandmother: wrinkled skin is soft and warm and waiting for a kiss and hug. But often all she gets are fists, splashed with salty tantrum tears; the ocean's just a sulking brat, like milk left sitting out too long. The island has unyielding arms that never panic in a storm; she holds the flailing violent child until she's finally calming down. It takes great strength to be so gentle, knowing every storm will pass, even if the calm is just the center of the hurricane. I am awed by how she still endures, ever constant year to year, the gentle slope is always there, her evergreen and mossy hair.

I walk around the Point again, as constant as the island is, following a pattern set by Jana back when we were kids. I trace along the jumbled logs, balancing as usual, careful not to let the logs snap vicious at a foot or shin. On the far side of the Point, there's Annie resting quietly, sitting like a rock on rock, hands on top her wooden cane. Her chin rests on her hands so it appears she's staring at the sea; eyes closed to the sunshine, though, that's splashing on her brilliantly. I can't recall the last time I saw Annie sitting out this far; usually she can't walk past the clothesline strung across her yard. It is obvious she sees the sunshine, pleasant look across her face; obvious she hears my footsteps, even though my feet are bare. My toes just whisper to the stone, but somehow she still knows I'm there; I imagine if it made a sound she'd hear the rising of the moon.

"Henry?" she says, to be polite.

"Hello, Annie," I say back.

I sit beside her on the rock, listen to the tiny waves, and it's nice to sit beside someone you know enjoys just sitting there. She doesn't say a word, but I can feel how much she likes the sound, the feel of wind across her face and messing up her thinning hair. All across one side of us, the sun is climbing through our clothes, rubbing up against our skin to counteract the freshened breeze. I know she likes it just like me, or else she wouldn't sit out here; and that all by itself is fine, makes sitting with her comfortable. We're close there but we do not touch, the rock she picked just big enough, and we listen to the island take the constant beating of the waves, feel the gentle sunshine rays, I watch the ferry make its way from Shannon Point to Horseshoe Bay.

She reaches out her hand just then and touches lightly on my arm, fingers wrap around my wrist so that she knows I'm listening. She tells me of a memory, three-quarters of a century: how, long ago, she used to sail out in the Inner Hebrides.

"I used to sail," she tells me, "out through islands very much like these." A little boat her father made, could carry maybe two or three. She'd lie out on the covered bow, listen to the flapping jib: absent-minded father-sailor wouldn't always pull it in. She still can hear the sound of swells that lapped against the wooden hull, how like a heartbeat that it was, although a bit irregular. She thought about the ocean, and how strong she thought her father was; and yet the ocean's being kind, could crush them with a flex of swell. Caressingly it brushed its lips up softly on the wooden boat and let them play on gentle currents, batted by the teasing winds. She'd felt the sun-shine on her face, felt the sea was so benign, tacking back and forth between the islands of the Hebrides. She loved to sail just like she loves to sit now on these solid rocks, listen to the beating waves, their reassuring energy. She never worried way back then, although she hadn't learned to swim: her father made the boat himself, had such a steady tiller hand.

"We talked," she said, of her and Jana, perhaps reminded of herself: her hair as black as Jana's then, when she was young and beautiful. "It's such a shame. I should have known. I once thought I might kill myself." Her hand still wrapped around my wrist: her father's tender tiller grip. Now her hair is silver-gray, like rocks along the island's shore: "But that was a long time ago. I'm lucky I got over it."

"How's Annie been?" my father asks, his mouth full of spaghetti sauce.

"Fine, I guess," I answer, taking seconds on the garlic bread.

"Did you get her mail today?"

"Doesn't come on Sundays."

"Good lord. I guess I'm way behind. Would have sworn that it was Saturday."

He takes another fork of noodles, twirls them in the sauce I'd made, followed by a bite of salad, croutons poured out of a box.

"I saw her on the Point," I say, "earlier this afternoon."

"She still goes out a bit, then? I thought she couldn't walk that far."

I'm thinking it's a little strange she suddenly should change her ways; it seems each time I walk the beach she's standing on the Point again. We'll sit and chat a little while, she'll ask for help back up the trail; it's just a couple hundred feet back to her little bungalow.

"I remember when I was a kid. She and the Doctor were just newlyweds—hanging on each other like a couple horny teenagers...." I push my plate back suddenly, then steal a momentary glance: my father's face was blushing red, embarrassed by the words he'd said. "I had a crush on her," he tells me, though he's looking out the window now. "She had the darkest eyes I'd ever seen. Seemed so full of life and energy. She was thirty years my senior, but was really rather beautiful."

"I suppose," I say, glancing away.

"She must be pretty lonely now. I can't imagine how she gets along."

"Just does, I guess," is all I say; get up to clear the plates away.

bushes bend
kiss fleshless bone
a lover lying in the grass
ghostly white and lonely though
the suffering done long ago
and last time I was up this trail, Jana held me by the
hand; I'm missing every stinging nettle, careful what I
step around. It's nice the way the sun streaks through,
splashing off the undergrowth: bitter-berried bushy
plants with leaves the size of dinner plates. It's all mag-
nificently thick, and every bit is green or brown; the only
other color's me, with red stripes on my tennis shoes.
I've got sneakers on and khaki shorts, a T-shirt that

I've worn for days; the light streaks through the upper story: Douglas firs and cedar trees. The sun flicks like a silent movie, splashing in my bleary eyes; it's jungle warm and humid and there's something I'm allergic to. My mom took me for testing once, back before I could refuse: painful patches on my back showed allergies to dust and mold. But every year there's something new: can't pet the neighbor's Persian cat; something blossomed in the woods is triggering an eye attack. My eyes are itchy-watery, I have to wipe them on my sleeve; haven't started sneezing yet, although my nose is tickling. I've talked about this trail before, how seldom it gets walked upon; it's just a disappearing road from when my father was a boy. I'm walking to the Doctor's lake, the sun blinks on and off my face, amazed the sun can penetrate through forest dense as chocolate cake.

Jana held my hand last time, her other brushed against the leaves, gently raking through the green, yet somehow missing nettle stings. Now I come out all alone into the clearing that we'd made; startling the sterile trees still wading to their naked knees. My eyes are driving me insane, so faucet-like they're watering; can barely see the rippling waves come scream across the Doctor's lake. I cringe and cover up my ears, brace against the puff of breeze, anticipating something more than just this little puppy sneeze. It cools the sweat on chest and arms, sways the long stems of the grass, no longer lying dry and flat where we made love so many times. I kick my shoes into the brush and drop my clothes off where I stand, imagining the touch of Jana's actively exploring hand. Wading in the chilly water, feet slide underneath the mud, can feel the buried sticks and twigs while wading till it's deep enough.

I cup my hands into the water, splashing cold onto my face, washing out the nasty dust of trees trying to propagate. The cold is soothing to my eyes, quiets down the burning itch; thigh deep in the water now my testicles begin to shrink. I lean into the water so I feel as if I'm swallowed up; plunge beneath the surface like I'm breaking through a skin of ice. For a moment all there is is cold—flooding both my ear canals, entering my mouth and nose, slowing all my molecules. And that moment while I'm well immersed I'm weightless as a puff of smoke; the noise of splashing through the surface very quickly dissipates. I open up my eyes and see the streaky light through murky brown; keeping still, the silence must be similar to being drowned. It's as if I've been transported out to someplace deep in outer space: I'm just a floating chunk of rock off drifting through the universe. This moment doesn't last too long, eventually I have to breathe; stumbling thrashing trying to stand in water reaches to my waist. My feet beneath the silky mud feel warmer than the rest of me; I'm wiping water off my face to try to get my bearings straight. I focus on the naked trees, standing with their branches stiff; suddenly occurs to me they're maybe doing Highland Dance. Their branches twist above their heads, with slender wrists and elbows bent; they likely could be dancing to some loud and droning bagpipe hymn. I think about the driftwood Annie showed me back a week ago: just a salty chunk of root she'd touched up with some sandpaper. Then once again I dive right in to swim around the dancing trees, racing heart and gasping chest, my mind numbs with the biting cold.

I push the grass down out of breath and prop my head against a log: I'm on my back, skin red and damp, still naked as the newly born. The sun warms all the sparkling drops of water on my abdomen; I'm looking down this great expanse of body I've inherited. My father hasn't any mass, he's skinny as a flower stalk; my mom's a nervous bird-like thing from dieting and working out. I haven't any siblings to compare how I'm developing, but in the last year and a half my body's metamorphosing. I'm staring down a broadened chest, there's muscle underneath the flesh; I'm not exactly Jack LaLanne, but I've got some well developed pecs. I have to pull my belly back to see the mound of pubic hair; Jana never said so but my penis seemed to work okay.

My thighs seem strong and muscular, my feet a half a mile from here; it's not the body of a man, but hinting that I'm getting there.

The sun has warmed me up so now my testicles are peeking out; and looking down I see a tiny ant crawl on my abdomen. I wonder if it's going to bite, to sink into my belly flesh; I load a finger on my thumb and flick the ant into the brush. A game that Jana used to play: she'd herd them on my lower back, race them up and down my spine to see how much I'd tolerate. I'd finally have to roll aside; she'd maybe do some oral sex, then climb on top, slide me inside, her teeth sunk in my willing neck. I'm looking at my penis now, still shrunken from my chilly swim; I wonder if I concentrate if I could get it up again. It's just a mental exercise, not really feeling in the mood; I pinch a bit of wrinkled skin and stretch to give it length and width. I've got the image in my head of Jana's slender naked hips; taking little tiny bites she nibbles on my frenulum. I'm thinking of the looks she'd flash, all sparkle-eyed and mischievous, and maybe for a couple beats, the blood pumps up my penis shaft. But no matter how I tug and pull, it barely reaches quarter mast; I can't suppress the image of her long hair in a tangled mass. I'm so glad that I wasn't there to see her underneath the waves; they found her floating face up in the water outside Cable Bay. They brought a dog named Rosy in, trained to find the floating dead; standing in the bow she's barking, sniffing at the passing wind. It's days since Jana disappeared, the storm had finally tuckered out; I'd watched them from the window as the search boat motored past the Point. Nobody described the scene, I made this up all by myself; I know they found her fully clothed, but that's not how I see her now. The picture that I've got is that she's three feet underneath the waves; every time a swell goes past her naked image undulates. I see her private pubic mound through water that is crystal clear; she's floating with her arms straight out like Jesus hanging on the cross. Her image shimmers with each wave, I see the scars above her breast, her long black hair a tangled mess that hides the look upon her face. I'm haunted by that hidden look, will never know her final thoughts: did Jana merely slip and fall or did she really kill herself.

Every time I touch myself this image of her interferes; the only reason that I try is morbid curiosity. I haven't got an ounce of lust, my penis just an ornament; I finally give up in disgust, just leave it hanging shriveled up. I think about the dog they had, this happy yellow Labrador: Rosy trained to trace the subtle essence of our rotting flesh. I watched her sniffing from the bow as they slowly motored past the Point; her trainer in a pleasant voice is giving her encouragement. I envy now this happy dog, so cheerful going at its job: her big tail wagging back and forth, oblivious and ignorant.

I'd fallen off to sleep and had a dream I still can clearly see; I'm lying naked in the grass, but up above the sky is gray. The tips of all the towering trees go flailing in a massive storm; down here the grass is nice and calm, a warm and pleasant atmosphere. I prop up on my elbows then, and look across the Doctor's lake, the sterile trees are dancing round, they're splashing like a bunch of kids. Their arms are just like jellyfish, they move them with a fluid grace; and suddenly they all just stop, aware that I am watching them. From the corner of my eye I see a deer walk from the stormy woods: a little doe with darkest eyes, her hide as clean and white as bone. And it's me now who can't move at all, and the white deer walks right up to me; the storm above my head is fierce, the booming thunder deafening. The little deer has come up close, its head just inches from my own; I feel it nudge me with its hoof, as solid as a billy club. That was all the dream there was, the deer just turned and walked away; and suddenly I've woken up, the sky no longer steely gray. I'm stupid from this sudden sleep, I get up from the itchy grass, walk into the water to wash straw from off my butt and back. With three quick steps I dive right in, I'm once more startled by the cold; I take a couple gasping strokes and turn around and climb back out. I feel the pounding of my heart, my nervous system's after-shock; I'm picking up my khaki shorts, my T-shirt used for drying off. I'm searching naked for the shoes I'd kicked off somewhere stupidly; looking over fallen logs and underneath the bushy leaves. I find one by a rotting stump, and have to brush the ants away; feel the touch of twigs and leaves against the insides of my legs. The other shoe went further off, and it's strange to feel so vulnerable; walking naked through the woods, more sensitive than usual. I feel the firmness of the ground, the touch of grass seed on my knee, can see the red stripe running round my other worn-out tennis shoe. I should have felt more startled finding where I find my shoe: resting on a pile of bones still bleaching in the afternoon.

I stand still in my nakedness, clothes still hanging from one hand; my shoe is resting on the deer we'd found dead back a year ago. At first I want to leave the shoe, so not to get close to the deer; the skeleton was scattered when some scavenger got into it. The bones are bleached a toothy white, the rib-cage all that's left intact; the rest is just a jumbled mess of vertebrae and scapulas. But I know I can't walk barefoot home, so I pick the shoe up carefully, trying not to move the bones, and so disturb the resting dead. I walk a ways into the woods before I put on shorts and shoes, my T-shirt smelling dank and damp while pulling it down past my nose. I'm not yet halfway home before my eyes begin to flush with tears, well before I pass the bush that's triggering my allergies.

the moon means nothing
really nothing
although it moves the ocean child
          tonight
the water barely sizzles
although
I know
she makes it boil
I see her standing on the Point, watch her throwing
something in; can't quite get it figured out, she's such
a frail, pathetic thing. The moon shines on the water so
it casts her into silhouette; she's leaning on her cane so
she's the image-perfect wicked witch. All she needs are

thirteen cats, swarming round her underfoot, but they don't come out on the rocks, too frightened by the water slap. Annie's standing all alone, it must be nearly twelve o'clock; I couldn't sleep and thought I might go watch the tide come in and out. I'm walking towards her in the dark, just the moonlight on the rocks, and she turns around and takes a step to lean against a massive log.

The log's been beached since I was born, and maybe forty years before; my father says he can't recall a time the landmark wasn't there. It must have been an angry storm that threw the old tree on the Point; tossed so far the highest tide now barely even touches it. Annie leans against this ancient monolithic behemoth, then rests her chin against her hands supported by her walking stick. I still can see the rippling circles spreading round what she threw in, as if the waxing yellow moon was dripping on a sea of glass. The ocean swells are smooth and wide, there's not the briefest puff of wind; the moon's at least three quarters full, a touch more than a day ago. I know her cats are waiting for her, hiding in the scrubby brush, hairless tails twitch back and forth each time the ocean slaps the rock. I think that Annie makes the moon rise, keeps her up so late at night; cats come out to watch her throw the sizzle on the ocean top. I'm walking toward her near the water, round the quiet tidal pools; listen to the tiny crabs climb through the cracks and crevices. I am certain she can hear me with my scuffing rubber sneaker soles, walking on the barnacles and tiny periwinkle snails. The ocean's sleeping soundly now all wrapped up in the island's arms; there's just the sound of sleepy breathing, thumping of its beating heart. But she doesn't greet me when I'm near, close enough to startle her; I see the moon gleam off her hand, her simple golden wedding band.

"Hello, Annie," I whisper, and she moves her head as if to see, then motions with her gleaming hand the space of log right next to her.

"Hello, Henry," she whispers back, so not to wake the sleeping child, indicating with her hand her invitation to sit down.

"I didn't hear you coming."

"I hope I didn't scare you, then."

"Heavens, no. I'm much too old. Nothing scares me anymore."

We lean ourselves against the log, as solid as a brick of lead; quiet as the moon still rising, constellations overhead. It is comfortable to sit beside her, knowing that she isn't scared; the darkness that she's in is just the darkness she's in anyway. She is pleased to sit out late at night, listen to the water breathe; pleased to have me come along to sit and keep her company. She must be awfully lonely now, with hardly any visitors: Mrs.

Bishop once a week brings bread and milk and groceries. My father had a crush on her, yet never goes to say hello; Jana used to fetch the mail, now I'm the one who does that chore. So I'm guessing that she thinks it fine I've come to share her sense of dark; surprised to find that, just as well, I'm glad that she was sitting there.

I'm breathing in the ocean air, tangy sweet and seaweedy, pungent briny cool and fresh as salad tossed with vinegar. I hold a pebble in my hand, picked up from a salty pond: wet and smooth and solid as the log that we are leaning on. If I held my hand open, the stone would glimmer in the moon, but I keep my fingers tight around it, smothered in my sweaty palm. Annie reaches out a hand, her fingers touch against my arm; she wraps them tight around my wrist, a momentary tenderness. Her hand then goes back to her cane, moon caught on her wedding band, and perhaps her darkness is just knowing that she is awake again. It is chilly even without breeze; I'm really not dressed properly: just a skinny T-shirt and a worn-out pair of dungarees. I wrap my arms around my chest, holding back what warmth I've got; I feel a chill start in-between my low back and my shoulder blades. She told me once the hard part was not knowing how to tell the time: wakes up from an evening nap, can't tell if it is eight o'clock or sometime middle-of-the-night. So she listens to the radio, while sitting in her easy chair, waiting for the songs to stop, the early morning station breaks.

"Do you always come out late at night?" and this was Annie asking me.

"Just when I can't get to sleep," which happens fairly frequently.

I'm looking at the water, with its gentle undulating swells, moon reflecting off the surface, black as looking down a well. I barely see the vaguest shape, whatever Annie threw away, floating out now twenty feet, the current sleeping lazily. I still don't recognize the shape, it could just be a piece of kelp; maybe she's embarrassed that I've caught her throwing garbage out.

"The moon must be quite nice tonight," and I try to tell her what it's like: full, perhaps, in three more days, a cookie with a single bite. And if not for the tidal slap, there's not too many other sounds: the constant scratch of crab on rock, a distant diesel rumbling. We hear it from a ways away, a fishing boat from Cable Bay, running navigation lights, returning to Port Angeles. The engine beat is droning steady, building as it's coming near, not too far off in the strait, a hypnotizing chug and ping. We're quiet as we listen to it, lonely as a midnight train; I see the cabin lights come on, but only momentarily. In my mind I see the pilot pouring from a thermos jug, sipping at it now and then to keep a steady coffee buzz. A diesel running late at night on water so molasses smooth, is lonely as the sound of wind when no one's there to share it with. It maybe takes five minutes for the fishing boat to disappear, far side of the Point and then around the island's southern end.

She told me then about a boy she knew back when she was my age, back when she was just a girl and spent summers in the Hebrides. A sweet young lad with long red hair who worked his father's fishing boat; just he and his dad went out, earned a living fair enough. He wrote her lines of poetry, rhyming little love letters; saw her only once each week right after Sunday services. One day his father brought him in, his foot caught in the fishing net; father couldn't frantic drag the massive net in fast enough.

"I had to throw them all away," the poems that he wrote for her. "I took a little row boat out and let the water swallow them."

I'd been trying to ignore the cold, the dew condensing on my clothes, but couldn't stop this shaking chill that suddenly sweeps over me. It shakes me uncontrollably, starting in my shoulder blades, rolling out in all directions, private little hurricane. It passes through my feet and hands, shakes the log we're leaning on; I'm certain Annie feels the tremor, wonders maybe something's wrong. I'm waiting for the sound of waves to loudly crash against the shore, listen for the sound that trees make crashing through the underbrush. But all stayed quiet as before, and Annie doesn't say a word, just listens to the distant boat, the fading diesel chug and ping.

She told me something then, although I can't remember what it was; I just remember feeling it was something truly wonderful. I had a sense of other-worldliness, the light from just the moon and stars, the smell the ocean makes at night, strong with rotting death and life. Maybe she was telling me ingredients for toxic brews, evil incantations and the secrets of the universe. I had my arms wrapped round my chest, leaning back against the log; every now and then she'd reach and touch a hand against my wrist. That gentle touch was reassuring, knowing that she's glad I'm there, glad to share this quiet time between her chore of changing tides. Whatever she was telling me, it didn't take her very long; suddenly she's quiet, then she's laughing for a little while. Perhaps it was a joke she told, I know I laughed along with her, maybe just to be polite or from a tickled funny bone. She pushes herself off the log then, brushing off the gritty sand, asks if I would walk her home, much safer with a steady hand. So I help her through the rocks and logs, through the trees and underbrush, listen to her ill-bred cats go scatter off ahead of us. I leave her at her cottage door, feel her fingers trace my cheek, listen to her walk inside, not bother flipping on the switch. As I walk back toward my house, our dark and quiet bungalow, I glance down on the ocean front, see something floating past the Point. I am not sure why it scares me, but I feel as if my heart has stopped; for a moment I think maybe it's a body floating belly up. Then suddenly it disappears, has left a spreading ripple ring: an otter or a harbor seal, out for a little midnight swim. And that's when it occurs to me, what Annie tossed in earlier; she's throwing back the wooden poems, driftwood sculptures no one's seen.

rattle-trap
and ankle-snap
brittle shell of fiberglass
organ-donor, gravel scrape
road-rash-rock from hands and face
I can't believe I'm doing this: biker-dude and biker-chick; barely makes it up the hill, my straining little scooter-bike. But she said she'd never been on one, so I offered her a little ride; let her wear my helmet since I didn't have an extra one. Her balance isn't good at first, she doesn't lean into the turns; but by the time we reach the road she's starting to get comfortable. She's sitting straddled on the back, my buttocks pinched between

her thighs; she's got her arms around my waist, her breasts against my shoulder blades. Each time I twist the throttle grip she squeezes out more of my breath; every time we hit a bump she giggles like a lunatic. My scooter doesn't go too fast, has hardly any giddyup; I'm nervous since I haven't ever had a rider on the back. But the one main road is nicely paved, a mix of curves and straight-a-ways, so once we're on macadam I try picking up a little speed.

I'm giving her a verbal tour, on the left's the Bishops' store; I have to shout so she can hear above the whine of second gear. We puttered past the golf-course, past the little church for Protestants, steep road leads off to the right goes straight down to the ferry dock. When I ask if she's afraid, she says *don't be ridiculous,* so coming round another curve, I twist the rubber throttle grip. My helmet's got a plastic shield that keeps the wind out of my eyes, but Annie's got the helmet on and I'm not wearing anything. I've nudged it up to thirty-five just as we crest a little hill; straight shot down the other side, I coax the scooter faster still. I'm thinking of the image in the picture that I stole from her, found it on a dusty shelf while she was making tea for two. She'd gone off to the kitchen, so I wandered round her living room, looking at the titles of the books she'll never read again. Way down on a lower shelf, an album full of photographs, the pictures held with little corners, pages stuck and bent in half. The photos are old fashioned ones, black and white and sepia: people dressed in Sunday best out standing by their Model Ts. The clothes they wore were sometime from the first half of the century: suits and ties and wide-brimmed hats, the dresses well below the knee. It was only vaguely interesting, these strangers long since passed away, backgrounds I imagined to be basic Scottish scenery. I was flipping through the pages when a single image caught my eye, portrait of a striking girl, looks maybe six- or seventeen. She was standing in some farmer's field, classic piles of straw and hay, mud caked to her rubber boots: peasant shirt and overalls. Her hair was long and wavy dark with freckles scattered round her nose; chin seemed faintly masculine, a slightly Mona Lisa smile. But the eyes were what had caught my own, all mischievous and full of mirth, almost like she's thinking of a joke she's playing on herself. I was fascinated by the eyes, the haunting little sexy smile; I tried to turn the album page, kept turning back to look at her. It was almost like this photograph had linked directly to my brain, stimulating neurons that were on the verge of atrophy. Then Annie's coming down the hall, the cups and saucers on a tray, rattled by the tremor that seemed worse with every passing day. I don't want her to know that I've been pawing through her private things; don't yet want to give up staring at this fading photograph. It's not like me to do these things, but I pulled it from the album page, stuck it in my pocket while I put her memories away.

Later on that afternoon, out on the rocks all by myself, I sit and try to figure out what made me swipe this photograph. It's not because it looks like Jana, Jana's hair was straight and black, eyes were further spaced apart, her skin was olive-smooth and dark. But something keeps me looking at it, eyes so bright and beautiful; linked directly through my brain down to my heart and genitals. It dawns on me this image is the first I've been attracted to; months since Jana passed away, I hadn't looked at anyone. I felt like I had had my chance, found my one true love and lost; suddenly I'm staring at a face could keep me up at night. It startles me that I could fall in love with some old photograph; no idea who it could be, with nothing written on the back. Of course she must be dead already, she's got to be a hundred now, buried in some Scottish grave-yard back a half a century. I'm trying to imagine what this girl would look like really old: wrinkled skin and graying hair, her eyes as bright as ever, though.

"I saw you down here all alone. I thought you'd maybe like a beer."

He's never once done this before, come down here

from his reading chair; my father just behind me with two bottles and an opener. At first I'm startled that he's there, caught me with the stolen goods; then I'm startled just as much he's offering me alcohol. The gesture isn't lost on me, acknowledging advancing age; wonder if he knows that I'll be twenty in another year. He sits down on the rock beside me, cap popped off a long-necked ale, tasting stout and slightly sweet, it cuts the thickness in my mouth.

"Thanks," I say, "I needed that," while trying to act nonchalant; the picture slipped into my pocket, sticking out a half an inch. He takes a few sips from his beer, looking at the tiny waves, watching as the ocean swells come rolling in from far away.

"You haven't had the boat out much. I had them tune the Evinrude."

"Haven't really had the time."

"Now that's a pretty lame excuse."

I had to laugh because I'm caught, time's about all that I've got. "I guess I haven't felt like it. Lonely out there by myself."

I'm waiting then for his response, I've never made a hint before; he takes another sip of beer and very slowly swallows it.

"I'll bet you miss her terribly," and that's not what I thought I'd hear; thought he'd maybe offer to go fishing in a couple days. I'm not sure how I should reply, words stuck halfway out my throat; tried to help them with a sip, but that just washed them down again.

"Your mother called this afternoon. Wanted me to talk to you. Guess she got your final grades. Barely made a two-point-oh."

I'm staring at the water now, I'm not sure what he wants from me; take another sip of beer, not focusing on anything.

"She told me I should ground you, but she doesn't really understand. I'm thinking you'll do better when you've had time to get over it."

The words still stuck down in my throat then felt like they were choking me; something on the breeze, perhaps, was cranking up my allergies. I feel a band around my chest, can't get my breath in all the way; never had much asthma, but I suddenly begin to wheeze. My father doesn't seem to notice, staring at the swelling sea, silent for the longest time, the beer at last relaxing me. I finally get a full breath in, still I haven't said a word.

"Let's go after dinner," he says. "See if we can catch some fish."

Then he asks to see the photograph, I can't think how I can refuse; he has to hold it out a ways, he'd left his glasses with his book. He stares at it the longest time, thoughtful as he sips his beer, squinting at the black and white, the details hadn't faded yet.

"It's no wonder I had such a crush. A face to launch a thousand ships." And he hands me back this photograph of Annie when her eyes were clear.

We crest the hill at thirty-five, and Annie's got me round the waist, seems the faster that I go, the louder Annie's laughter gets. The wind is blasting in my eyes, creeping up to forty-five, wonder how much fun she was when she was just a tender lass. Through my windswept bleary eyes I see the southern coast of France, puttering my Vespa scooter through the steep Italian Alps. We're eating in sidewalk cafes, cheap hotels with balconies, sunlight blows the curtains as we sleep straight through the afternoons. I watch her hips and shoulders as she's diving off a wooden dock, cutting through the deep blue of a lonely Grecian swimming beach. I barely see the road ahead, squinting through my windburned eyes; tears blow from the outside corners, Annie's squeezing tight behind. We're topping out at fifty as we reach the bottom of the hill; can't let go to wipe my eyes, the front wheel isn't balanced right. I know the island well enough, the road curves sharply to the left; I lean into the corner then but Annie does the opposite. I'm pushing on the pedal brake, front wheel starts to wobble shake, slides into the gravel where the blacktop fades to dirt and dust. I haven't yet lost all control, leaning more to compensate; I get the wheels back on the road, so glad they steeply banked the curve. I bring the scooter to a stop, I'd nearly killed the two of us; trembling hands and beating heart I cut the whining engine off. Annie's laughing out of breath, says she's had an accident.

"I laughed so hard I peed my pants. It might be time to take me back."

eyes impaled

on photograph

universal joint and shaft

can't quite get

the image right

strangled in the sheets at night

      two o'clock

      wide awake

      tide keeps going

      in and out

wrist begins to stiff and ache

venom of a poisoned snake

I find her working in the yard, yanking on the garden
weeds: Mrs. Borden, Jana's mom, lonely since her daugh-

ter's gone. I've been by once or twice before, awkwardly to say hello; her son comes now on Sunday nights for dinner and a video. She acts so glad to see me that it makes me wonder if it's real; tells me just how nice I am for thinking of her now and then. She never speaks of Jana, like she's not the reason that I'm there: just a sad look on her face, her heart about to melt away. I can't stand staying very long, sensing Jana's mother's love; feeling guilty that I didn't tell her something soon enough.

"Let me make some lemonade. It's too hot standing in the sun."

She leads me through the side door where I carried Jana long ago, stopped before the freezer where she finds the frozen lemonade. I ask to use the bathroom while she's running water in the sink, tells me that I know the way, down the hall and to the left. I haven't been inside the house since helping Jana load her things: dragged her trunk out to the car all college-bound and oil-leaks. She seemed then only slightly strange, just quieter than usual; didn't want us waiting with her at the ferry terminal. So the last time that I saw her she had given Mom a kiss goodbye, wrapped her arms around my neck, left my cheek and earlobe wet. The car her brother gave her made a smelly cloud of blue exhaust, mixing for a moment with the tang of rotting kelp and moss. I still can hear the crunch and pop of gravel underneath

the tires; Jana going off to college, Mrs. Borden's teary
smile. Her mom asked if I'd come inside, but I told her
I had chores to do; spent the last few days of summer
wandering the rocky shore.

Now I'm walking down the hall, past the door to
Jana's room, heading for the bathroom where I'm hoping
to relieve myself. But I'm not prepared for what's among
the tile and linoleum: the smell of Jana's just-washed hair,
the scent of Jana's flesh and bones. I have to stand there
for a while before the open toilet bowl; can't quite make
myself relax with Jana standing next to me. I wash my
hands with Jana's soap, amazed how much it smells like
her; dry my hands against a towel smells like her clothes
and underwear. I look inside one of the drawers to see
what brand of soap is there; open up the mirrored door,
the medicines and razor blades. I'm not sure what I'm
looking for, signs of Jana's private life: what she used to
shave her pits, clippers for her fingernails. The top shelf
of the cabinet's full of bottles printed with her name;
wonder why her mother hasn't cleaned the cabinet of
her things. There are six or seven plastic bottles filled
with different medicines; dates go back for several years,
never threw out anything. I'm reading the prescription
labels, pharmacy in Bellingham: Prozac, Zoloft, Ativan;
lithium and thorazine. Half say that they're for depression, others say they're sleeping pills; supposed to take

these in the morning, others she should take with food. I twist the cap off each of them, look down at the medicines: blue and yellow, white and red; string them, wear them round your neck. Each small plastic bottle's got a good supply of pills inside; seems like Jana only tried each flavor maybe once or twice. Almost like it's habit forming, swiping things from people's homes; I pour the pills out in my hand, makes a hefty little hill. Each pill's almost beautiful, capsules glossy gelatin; I wrap them up in toilet paper, careful as I pocket them. I put the empty bottles back, hope her mom's not keeping track; flush the toilet, drop the seat, fold the towel nice and neat. As I step into the hall, I hear the noise a blender makes: Mrs. Borden in the kitchen stirring up the concentrate.

Jana's bedroom's two steps down, door is just a touch ajar; hoping just to take a peak, I push it with my fingertips. Grandma's quilt's still on the bed, pillows plumped up at the head; everything the way it was except her mother's cleaned the mess. The door swings open silently, inviting me to step inside; entering the sanctuary, first time since we said goodbye. She never put up any posters, pictures pulled from magazines; just one photo of her father, handsome rugged fisherman. Jana shared his dark set eyes, sparkling with intelligence; I pick the picture from the dresser, wonder what the man was like. All that time I'd thought his death was just a freakish accident; wonder what made him decide he's better off to kill himself. In my bulging pocket now there's evidence of something wrong; Jana's death was just a flaw she'd gotten from her father's side. I wonder what his note had said, tucked inside his favorite book; how could he have justified the anguish of his sudden death. I sit then on her well-made bed, hand placed on her mattress dent; thinking maybe it would help if she had also left a note. I'm staring round her bedroom when the obvious occurs to me; the south wall's covered thick with books, an old encyclopedia.

I squat down there before the shelves, brightly painted bookcases, filled with children's picture books and texts of high-school algebra. I realize I've no idea if Jana had a favorite; remember that she liked to read, but only when it's raining out. There's a paperback of *Moby Dick*, with sections underlined in ink; I'm thinking of her father's death, a different boating accident. But nothing's stuck between the pages, note explaining why she left; I put the book back on the shelf, start flipping through another one. I'm going through them randomly, fanning pages upside-down: Doris Lessing, Doctor Seuss, dog-eared stack of Nancy Drew.

"I've been through every one of them," and Mrs. Borden's standing there, clenched in each her sorrowed fists a sweating glass of lemonade. But she doesn't show that she's upset I'm snooping through her daughter's things; she acts as if I have the right to wonder why she'd killed herself. She sits beside me on the bed, handing me the drink she'd made; finally when she starts to speak, her voice is sadly gentle-sweet.

"I know I should have told you this. I wasn't being fair to you. You were practically her only friend, so I didn't want you scared away."

"I should have told you Jana had been seeing a psychiatrist," who gave her pills she never took, couldn't do much more than that. Jana cycled on and off, sometimes happy, sometimes not; different boyfriend every week, got her into trouble once. "For three months she'd be doing fine, first or second in her class," next report card barely passed, always acting out in class. "Then suddenly she's so depressed I have to keep her home from school," she can't quite make herself get dressed, mornings she'd just lie in bed. She lost all of her grade school friends, times when she'd insulted them; had them check her once for drugs, her urine test was negative. She's not sure what effect I had, but summers were her stable time; all her other boyfriends just the short-term, take-advantage kind.

"I thought that if you knew all this, you wouldn't want her hanging round. I know that you were good for her. I guess I wasn't thinking clear."

I'm swimming in a sea of guilt, motion-sick and short of breath; feeling like I've just been kicked, bleeding spleen and pancreas.

"I've searched the whole house for a note. I've gone through every single book. I know that Jana killed herself; she'd tried once with an overdose."

I wonder if I knew all this, would I have done things differently? Yanked her hands out of my pants? Told her she should go get lost? And her mother now is telling me of all the boyfriends that she had; expecting next she'll tell me I should go get checked for syphilis. It's like I didn't know her daughter, modern form of Jekyll/Hyde; wonder if she even liked me, last one left for her to bang. Mrs. Borden's sweet and kind—wish my mom was half as nice—but all I want is out of there, to get the hell away from her. I'm gulping down my lemonade, headache like you won't believe; hand her back the empty glass, tell her that I have to leave. I nearly stumble down the hall, neglect to kiss her mom goodbye; not sure where I'm supposed to go to re-invent my memories.

I'm trying to recall their names—blue and white was thorazine?—looking at the tiny numbers chiseled in the medicines. But I can't remember which was which, the kind to take if you're depressed, what would happen if I were to swallow one or two of each.

I've got them laid out on the tissue, lying on the flat-tened grass, pushed them into separate piles, semi-precious little jewels. They really are quite beautiful, sculpted surface shiny smooth, yellow one side, red the other: oval, round, triangular. The capsules have translucent covers, filled with multicolored beads; safety band around their middles, keeps them safe from tampering. It's common-knowledge pills are bitter, part of why they're good for you; every one a different color, hard deciding which to choose. I'm lying near the Doctor's lake, best place that I know to hide; wondering where Jana'd be if she had taken all of these. Would she have turned all nice and sweet and filled with healthy energy? Or would she have been lost and slow, yellow-eyed and zombie-dull? Or maybe it was for the best to let her be the way she was, bounding through her random orbit, crashing every now and then. Perhaps her fuse was short and fast, someone not designed to last, why she some-times couldn't stop, couldn't get to sleep at night. She had to pack the time she had, knowing it's not infi-nite; life was short and sometimes sweet: a suicidal maniac. The pills that she refused to take now glisten in the midday sun; pounding heart and sweating palms, I place a green one on my tongue. The feeling's vaguely sexual, standing on a jagged cliff, knowing

I could easy slip, tumble to a certain death. Yet I'm standing on the verge of death, maybe tempting destiny; tongue so dry the pill just sits there, not sure I can swallow it. It takes at least a couple moments for the taste to register, nasty caustic bitter-sour, squirting salivary glands. I think I'm going to swallow, but the pill gets caught not halfway down, feels as if it's trapped between my tonsils and the punching bag. I haven't got a water glass to wash the tablet further back, got it down just far enough to make me start to choke and gag. I gasping cough the tablet out, spit the taste out of my mouth; figure now I know the reason Jana left them on the shelf. I'm not sure what I thought would happen, taking just a single pill; need a gallon glass of water to take enough to really help.

making light
of drudgery
twice as many hands as eyes
fingertips to trace the grain
interdigitate at times

> some are buildings
>
> some are ships
>
> sinking, floating
>
> boats and bricks

sometimes happy
sometimes sad
laughing like a lunatic
Annie's got another piece, sitting near the pot of tea;
looks just like a sailing schooner if I don't look critically.

She wants help launching this as well, driftwood taken from a shelf; delivering her mail now takes up half of every afternoon. She has to tell me all their names, show me what was sanded smooth, holds me by the elbow as we slowly walk across the yard. She'll lean herself against a rock, listen for the sound they make, crashing through the wind and waves, finally back from where they came.

"I've got to tell you something," and she'll grab me by the wrist again, acting like she's serious but can't control a wicked grin.

"Sam and I were sailing once, right out here just off the Point. Suddenly the wind just dropped, couldn't feel a single puff."

She told me how they floated there, neither saying anything; told me how the sun was blazing, wished she'd brought her bathing suit. After what seemed half an hour, the Doctor started fidgeting; pulling out a half a dollar, tossed the coin into the sea. The sound it made was just the same as the driftwood I'd just tossed away: "solid as a hatchet, when you sink it in a cedar tree."

"And all at once the wind came up, nearly tipped us overboard. Samuel had to scramble quick to get the sails adjusted right."

I'm halfway through the flavors now, last night was the pink and green; funny how the different colors still all seem to taste the same. Once my father goes to bed, I pull the plastic baggie out; wasn't sure the toilet paper'd keep the pills quite fresh enough. I think it's an experiment, testing Jana's medicines; mostly they just make me sleepy, sometimes don't do anything. But last night I had dreams that made me want to try that pill again, vivid scene of God and Jana, playing checkers on my bed. I was standing next to Jana when I notice God's not doing well, Jana's got him set up so she'll jump him half a dozen times. I know it's God because he's got a bright light shining round his head; Jana knows she's got him beat, beaming with self-confidence. While she's waiting for her turn, she slips her hand inside my pants; right in front of God she takes my penis deep inside her mouth. I couldn't help but start to laugh, she's somehow tickling with her tongue; God just stares down at the board, can't figure how he'll win this one. I woke up with a pounding heart, a sticky mess between my legs; fell asleep and dreamed again of how the dog found Jana dead. She's just as I imagined her, naked underneath the waves; every time a swell goes past her image slowly undulates. But this time I can see her face, black hair floating all around; suddenly she winks and smiles, lets me know she's still alive. Next thing that I know I'm late, I'd slept right through my buzz alarm; asking why I'm not at work, my father shakes me by the arm.

Jumping straight up out of bed, feeling totally confused; naked grabbing for my clothes, jeans I've worn a week or two. Thanking Dad for waking me, I rush out to my scooter bike, wonder if they'll let me go for being forty minutes late.

At the time I'm thinking that I'll not repeat the pink and green; but now it's dark and late at night, I'm tempted by the vivid dreams. I'm looking at the tiny pill, funny fluffy pillow shape; toss it underneath my tongue, take a sip and swallow it. I'm lying on my bed next to a window screened and opened wide, listening to cricket sounds, the lapping of the midnight tide. Any moment now I figure I'll be falling fast asleep, visiting with God and Jana, now I know she's faking it. I'm lying on my back and have my arms held straight against my sides; any second now I should be trundled off to slumber land. The cricket sounds get louder, and the waves still beat against the shore; my eyes adjusting to the darkness, looking outside at the stars. It hasn't rained in several days, sky outside is crystal clear, stars as bright as lightning bolts, ground and scattered everywhere. After maybe fifteen minutes, I haven't even closed my eyes; I wonder if I shouldn't maybe try a bigger dose tonight. So I reach under the mattress where I keep the little plastic bag; decide to keep the light off so my father doesn't notice it. Searching through the bag of pills by light from other galaxies, I think I find the one that's right, but mostly by the way it feels. I have to swallow this one dry, I'm not sure where my glass has gone; stash the baggie out of sight, my head back on my pillow case.

Maybe it's been twenty minutes, maybe it's been half an hour, maybe just a moment but I still can't get my eyes to close. I'm staring out the open window, looking at the Milky Way; awesome when the moon is down how bright the universe can be. I search for constellations, ones that Jana taught me long ago, feel a sense of apprehension, sleeplessness anxiety. Maybe it was blue and yellow that I swallowed yesterday; could be that I misremembered, tripping now on Jana's speed. I'm thinking I should go and stick a finger down my stupid throat; don't know what I'm doing, maybe slowly poisoning myself. I'm just about to get up when I hear the distant snap of twig; listen for a moment thinking maybe I've imagined it. But there it is again, I think; someone's down there in the yard; must be Annie walking late, lost and stumbling in the dark. Then I hear the ping of pebble striking softly on the screen, the signal Jana used to use to wake me for a midnight fling. Suddenly I'm in the yard, standing right in front of her; in my dream the day before she'd told me she was still alive. She's living with her father, maybe, eating roots and little squirrels;

somewhere on the island they've been hiding from us all along. I'm not sure what I'm supposed to do, hug or walk away from her; Jana reaches up a hand, runs her fingers through my hair. The moon then comes up all at once, brightening the rocks and yard; moonlight on her naked chest shows all the scars have multiplied. I want to soothe the angry skin, touch them with my fingertips; want to be there always so it doesn't happen yet again. All at once we're making love, sex all sweaty glorious; right there where my father sits and reads his sorry paperbacks. As we're just about to climax, perfect simultaneous, father grabs me by the shoulder, once again I'm late for work.

"Won't be getting any raises, coming in late every day," and I'm jumping out of bed and grab the same clothes I wore yesterday.

He tells me I've got one more chance, plenty others want my job; not much work here on the island, otherwise he's satisfied. I come home late that afternoon, making up for time I'd lost, hoping that my job's secure, a couple weeks of summer yet. I'm walking down the Doctor's road, bringing Annie's daily mail; just a single letter from her lawyer off in Bellingham. She'd asked me not to open any till I've told her who they're from; never lets me read the ones that might seem somewhat interesting. Maybe folded up inside is her final will and testament; maybe she's decided that she'll leave me everything she's got. Then I wouldn't have to sweat the loss of boring, low-wage summer jobs; wouldn't have to listen to the windy lectures of my boss. Her cottage isn't very big, but the property is worth a lot; must have thirty-forty acres, only sand the island's got. I'm not sure she has next-of-kin, though someone's sure to claim to be: second cousin, thrice removed; mother's sister's daughter's kid .

I'm worrying about her some, it often seems she's not all there; starting to repeat herself, calls me by her husband's name. Doctor Samuel So-and-so, prominent pathologist; made a name when he was young by classifying liver cysts. She told me that at least three times while sipping just one cup of tea; other times she's razor sharp, full of jokes and subtleties. But more and more I'll find her in a blouse she's got on wrong-side-out; bet she spends a half-an-hour guessing how to button it. I made her dinner yesterday, I'm getting to be quite a cook; sat and watched her snarf it down, can't remember eating lunch. Since she's blind she has to eat with one hand resting on her plate, fingers have to touch the food so she can snag it with her fork. It's not always a pretty sight, watching while she eats her food: pasta puttanesca and then chocolate pudding for dessert.

I see her outside doing chores, a hundred yards ahead of me; she's hanging up her laundry from a basket comes up to her knees. She's made a little line of stockings, hung a couple stout braziers; not a touch of silk or lace, just mercenary undergear. Now she's got a cotton dress she's hanging on the sagging line; clothespin to one shoulder while she's reaching for another one. The wind is brisk and lifts a sleeve, then drops it lightly round her neck; have to laugh because it looks just like she's dancing with her dress. She bends to grab a light green blouse, stands to pin it to the line; suddenly she drops just like an apple from an apple tree. I'm running almost instantly, a record fifty-meter dash, knowing that I'll find her dead: a sudden massive heart attack. I'm kneeling in the grass beside her, lying with her left side down; carefully I turn her over, thinking about CPR. I take her wrist to find a pulse, her arm as limp as toast in milk; I bend close just as I'd been taught, look and listen for her breath. I feel it soft against my cheek, see her chest wall rise and fall, watch her right arm start to move, searching blindly through the grass. Then I say I'll be right back, I'm going to call the ambulance; her right arm quickly reaches out and grabs a handful of my shirt. She holds me there for quite a while, with more strength than I thought she'd have;

doesn't speak for several moments, breathing getting deeper though.

"They'll only make a fuss," she says, "I'm sure I just stood up too fast," and she wouldn't let go of my shirt until I promised not to call.

"Just help me get into the house," and it takes some time to get her there; left side doesn't work so well, but better after several steps. I help her over to the couch, put pillows underneath her head; she rests there with her eyes closed while I rush to get a water glass. I'm only gone a moment, but she's better by the time I'm back; some color finally in her face, her left arm showing signs of life.

"Dana Bishop had me see her doctor up in Bellingham. All that he could tell me was that I should take some aspirin."

I asked if I could get her some, she said she took it earlier; really feeling better now, strength back in her leg and arm. I'm not sure what I'm supposed to do, this seems like an emergency; tells me now she thinks she's fine, *you might as well go make some tea.* I don't think I should leave her, but it's tea she seems to like the best; I go into the kitchen where I quickly heat the pot and cups. I'm gone perhaps five minutes, and she's sitting up when I return, fondling with both her hands a piece of driftwood sanded smooth.

"Thank you, dear, that's sweet of you," she hears me put the teacups down. "And Sam, I don't think we should wait. I want them all thrown back tonight."

vacant-eyed religious cult

pining unrequited love

briefly postured derrieres

ventilating outhouse doors

  little tasteless Christmas cookies

    crescent-shaped with cinnamon

  maniacs and lunatics

    howling middle-of-the-night

sold from trunks of dusty cars

pocked by careless meteors

torturing the weaker gender

bloating cramping uterus

what then will the earth do when

there's no one left to raise the moon?

cast the shimmer on the water?

bake the poison cookie dough?

I'm sitting with my father where he likes to sit and read his books: ledge looks out across the water, sunny through the afternoon. I'm listening to ocean sounds, seagulls crying overhead, every now and then I hear my father turn another page. It's blue sky hot and beautiful; a week before I have to leave, to spend a couple days with Mom, then back to university. There's not a thing on this agenda even has a slight appeal: go to dinner with my mother, listen to her lecture me. I'm signed up for a single on an all-male dormitory floor; didn't want to share a room, but didn't want to be alone. Now that seems the last place where I'd like to spend my study time: listening to jocks and geeks at war with blasting stereos.

My father puts his book down then, drops it underneath his chair, lets a sigh out I can hear, turns his head to look at me. I was staring down at Annie's yard, needs someone to mow the lawn, a pathway through the long grass made from carting driftwood to the Point. I glance up at my father with the sense that maybe something's wrong: maybe the marina called to tell me that I've lost my job.

"How's your girl-friend doing?" and I know it's just his awkward joke, asking after Annie down there lonely living by herself.

"I think she had some kind of stroke," and he doesn't act a bit surprised, just chews an edge of finger-nail, doesn't answer for a while.

"I've been wondering about your plans. School starts in a week or two. If I were you I'm not sure I'd be ready to go back so soon."

I can't tell what he's thinking since he's constantly surprising me; several times this summer caught him staring at me silently.

"I was your age when my father died. Dropped dead of a heart attack. I took a whole year off from school. Couldn't seem to concentrate."

"I've been thinking about staying here," it's out before I've thought it through. "John says I could work until November if I wanted to."

I'm looking at him watch the grass, chew another fingernail; never talked about his father, just that he died long ago.

"Your mom's not going to like this," but I'm not sure that he really cares; can't say that I blame him since she doesn't treat him very well.

"I'll tell you what I'll do," he says, glancing at me from the grass. "Let me visit weekends, and I'll pay the phone and power bills."

It's quiet on the Promenade, sunset on the other side; every day gets darker sooner, summer finally running dry. I'm thinking as I walk along how really big the island is; just a geologic speck, but still a lot of dirt and rock. The Promenade is cluttered thick with boulders large as compact cars; rocks the ocean couldn't lift, even at its angriest. Scattered on the island there are still some stands of virgin trees, trunks so fat it takes a map and compass just to walk around. The Bluffs have got a view that some have come a thousand miles to see: watch the rip tide gallop past the entrance into Cable Bay. The island's eight miles long and has a highway with no yellow line; the only traffic happens when the ferries come exchanging cars. I can't think what more I could want, certain nothing that I need; wonder how long I could live and make excuses not to leave. I'm wondering how Annie feels, she's been here almost all her life, living as a simple housewife, married to a man she likes. She worked at raising vegetables, but didn't have a family; husband died a painful death from cancer of the pancreas. I can't tell if she's sorry that she didn't ever bear a child, doesn't have a son or daughter, dinner every Sunday night. Now she sits and listens to the music on the radio, waiting for the station breaks so she can know what time it is.

I feel a gripping jealous guilt still every time I think of this: who would Jana's child have been, the trouble some boy got her in? How would life be different if they hadn't scraped her uterus? Could she have been pregnant when deciding she would kill herself? There could have been a little Jana, tiny person tucked inside; little boy, slightly pudgy, maybe looks a bit like me. I've walked now till it's good and dark, the sky's been beaten black and blue; passing Jana's mother's yard, lights on in the dining room. Mrs. Borden's got a dish of something steaming in her hands, coming from the kitchen with her waist wrapped in an apron. Her son is sitting at the table, guess it must be Sunday night, must be over thirty but he hasn't gotten married yet. She puts the steaming dish down on a trivet near the centerpiece, takes her apron off and hangs it careless on her wooden chair. As she scoots the chair up, I can see the apron start to fall; sliding off the wooden rung, gently wafting to the floor. All it is is eating dinner, only family that she has; suddenly embarrassed to be spying in so blatantly. I'm standing in the darkened yard, had early dinner with my dad; Jana's mom might look up now, frightened by a Peeping Tom. I turn back down the Promenade, try to walk off nonchalant; don't want her to look up, see a stranger's shadow slinking off.

Every day she's more confused, she sometimes doesn't know my voice; I'm with her every afternoon, as soon as I get home from work. But once I get her oriented, let her know the time and day, maybe for a couple hours she'll seem just like herself again. We'll listen to the radio, she'll ask me to read from a book; slowly walk out through the yard, sit out on the sunny Point. We're almost through the driftwood now, every day a couple more; she always seems delighted when we're throwing back the art she made. She'll grab me once more by the arm, acting like she's serious; tell me yet the same old joke she's told so many times before. I find it strange that every time she tells the joke it's funnier; seems like every stick thrown back just makes her burden easier.

"Have I told you 'bout the married couples, who want to join this special church?" and she'll end up with the punch line of the cabbage and the grocery clerk.

We've been going very slowly through her albums full of photographs; sitting on the sofa, Annie telling stories on herself. Every photo in the album has a little anecdote: Annie, back when she was seven, first time falling off a horse. Then Annie at a formal dance, says it's like a high school prom: pretty in a sleeveless dress, showing off her collar bones. I start describing every picture, faces and the style of clothes; doesn't take her long to know exactly which I'm staring at.

"That one is my mother, and beside her is my auntie Jo. She used to date an Irish fellow, had such a funny looking nose."

We came then to the page I took the picture from

some weeks before; closed my eyes and tried then to describe it straight from memory.

"It's a girl, she's maybe seventeen, standing near a stack of hay. Her hair is long and straight and black, holds a pitchfork in her hands."

"I think you need to clean your glasses. I'd swear my hair was curly then." I don't know what I'm supposed to say; I'd mixed my memories again.

The stars are just incredible, a solid band of Milky Way; I'm sitting on the Ansleys' cliff with constellations everywhere. I'm trying to imagine all these people back in history, out late in their togas making pictures out of fantasy. There are bulls and bears and dragons up there, mighty twins with belted swords; barely can recall their names, much less which dots connect their forms. I can't believe how warm it is, the first week in October now; should be cold and raining but there's been a dry and balmy spell. I'm wrapped up in a coat and hat, dew condensing on my pants; still I'm feeling warm enough to star-gaze in the stubby grass. The stars seem close enough to touch, bright enough to read my watch; scattered lights so crystal sharp they have a three-dimension look. It overwhelms me then to think the stars aren't really close at all; the earth so small we see the stars, but no one out there's seeing us.

I'm thinking about Annie, how she had another of her spells; walking late the other night, I noticed that her lights were on. I didn't think much of it, but the light came through the open door; I thought the wind had blown it open, went to quietly pull it shut. There wasn't any music playing, guessing that she'd gone to bed; thought I'd turn her lights off for her, save on the electric bill. The screen creaked as I stepped inside, light on by the couch and chair; Annie's sleeping on the sofa, lying rather awkwardly. She says she likes the lights for warmth, still can see the shadows some; figure I should wake her up, let her know what time it is. She's awake before I reach her, though; for once, she doesn't call me Sam; reaches out her right arm, with her left arm folded under her.

"Henry, is it very late?" and I'm not sure what she means by that; I tell her that it's after midnight, creeping up on one o'clock. She thinks she's been like this for hours, left side isn't working right; asks me if I'll help her up, tuck her into bed tonight. She hasn't any strength at all, I have to hold her in my arms; feel her breath warm on my neck as shallow as a butterfly's. I carry her into the bedroom, unsure if she's still awake; put her in between the sheets, her left arm feeling weak and limp. As I'm just about to leave, she whispers in the smallest voice:

"Henry, promise not to tell. Don't go calling anyone."

I didn't close her bedroom door, didn't feel like I could leave; sat down on her sofa hoping maybe rest would help me think. The next thing I am waking from a sweetly sound and dreamless sleep; spent the night in Annie's house, slept there just the two of us.

I'm still not sure what I should do, lying watching stars tonight; by morning Annie had improved, moves her left side by herself. But she hasn't got the strength to walk, took her to the toilet twice; she told me just to step outside, she'd call me if she needed help. I'm not sure what I'm doing, playing nursemaid to the widow-witch; stopped correcting her each time she calls me by the Doctor's name. I called to the marina, told a lie that I was feeling sick; made us both a breakfast out of oatmeal and two-percent. Her cheer seems strangely natural, I'm watching as she fades away; I nearly choke each time she tries to tell her joke to me again. Then later in the afternoon, we got her photo album out: Annie and the Doctor back when they were grinning newly-weds. There's Annie weeding in the garden, cabbage size of bowling balls; shocked to recognize my father: Annie with the neighbor boy. I'm fascinated watching as I realize she's growing old; pictures change from

black-and-white to slowly fading Kodachrome. The last
one in the album was still taken twenty years ago; the
Doctor put his camera down when Annie's eyes began
to fail. He's got his arms around his bride, been married
maybe forty years; a glowing sparkle in his eyes, looks
at his wife adoringly. Already she's a stately lady, fea-
tures I now recognize: her slightly sagging cheeky jowls,
the extra flesh across her nose. But her hair was only
streaked with gray, not so densely wrinkled skin; looks
straight at me through the camera, the woman Jana
could have been.

I'm lying on my back now as I'm staring at the scattered stars, wonder how they'll punish me when Annie
finally passes on. I feel like an accomplice, somehow,
partner in some heinous crime; feels just like I'm
helping her commit slow-motion suicide. But I know it's
really Annie speaking, periods of lucency; doesn't want
the ambulance, or someone pounding on her chest. A
blue light streaks across the sky then, third one that I've
seen tonight: whisper of a shooting star, blazing grain
of meteor. These moments couldn't happen twice, coincidence can change your life: the star had barely faded
when I felt the earth begin to shake. It lasted just a couple
seconds, could have missed it easily; quickly sitting up
I'm tensed and waiting for the aftershock. I'm thinking

I should call my mom, she's terrified of shaking earth; last one that we felt I had to hold her till she settled down. I'm waiting for the second round, staring off across the Point, thinking about seismic scale and where the epicenter was. And that was when I saw the glow off somewhere over Arlington, suddenly I'm scared to death, my blood full of adrenaline. It couldn't happen just like that, fire couldn't spread so fast; maybe it's just city lights, half the population up. But I've never seen this glow before, spreading like a mushroom cloud; someone finally pushed the button, detonating arms device. I can't tell if my heart stopped or is beating at the speed of light, thinking maybe this is it, the last page of the history books. The glow has grown so bright and round, reflecting off the ocean's skin, it outlines someone on the Point, a figure in a flowing dress. I know exactly who it is, standing right where she went in; Jana's ghost has come to watch the end of all the rest of us. She holds her arms both raised up high, orchestrates the spreading glow, raising up this golden orb that's turns out to be just the moon.

I can't think when my last breath was, so I fill my lungs again with air; I taste the kelpy ocean breeze, the fragrant tang of cedar trees. And I'm ready to go back to school, catch the start of winter term; been through quite enough to change my major now to poetry. My heart has finally settled down, I've figured out what's going on: it's Annie out to raise the moon, a chore she'll likely always do.

Acknowledgements
January 7, 2011

The first time I finished this novel was in the early 1980s. It was an idyllic time. Beth and I were not-yet married, both twenty-three and just out of college, living in a tiny coconut-wood hut on a remote island in the South Pacific. I spent my mornings writing on an old portable typewriter, a clacking manual that was to the modern laptop what a donkey cart is to a pogo-stick.* By noon each day, I couldn't write another word, and would walk to the island's reef to snorkel the clear water until Beth was due home from her work as a Peace Corps volunteer. After many months I pulled the last page from the typewriter. We celebrated by pedaling our one-speeds to the local carry-out shack to share a $2 plate of purple yams with sautéed octopus legs. Soon after, at sunrise on an early morning climb to the top of

*Very different, but neither one gets you where you're going very fast.

an island volcano, Beth whispered, "Ask me now," and so I promptly and enthusiastically proposed. We had almost no money or possessions, but felt incredibly rich in life and love.

I've finished this novel several times since then, and a couple other books in-between. This last (and final) version comes less than three years after Beth passed away from a rare and incurable cancer at the age of fifty. A talented and accomplished writer herself, Beth Epstein Danner was always my greatest supporter and a tireless champion for my writing. Without her I would never have found my voice, and never would have written my books. Now, without her, I take inspiration from the memory of Beth's true and magnificent love and her short but wonderful life.

—CJD

January 5, 2013